The Deeper Game

Reading order

The Deeper Game

THE BANK ROBBERS BOOK 3

ANNIKA MARTIN

Chapter One

THOR, ODIN, AND I WERE NESTLED LIKE THREE PEAS IN A pod in the front seat of our souped-up Lincoln Navigator.

The SUV's giant size and dark-tinted windows would've made it the perfect vehicle if the three of us had wanted to do something fun.

But no, we were not doing anything fun.

We were doing something boring—staking out the Prime Royale Bank of Beverly Hills.

Which meant we had to watch it.

And watch it.

And watch it some more.

I rested my head on Thor's shoulder, enjoying the feel of his longish blond curls against my cheek. His muscular shoulder flexed as he played WhatWord on his iPad.

It was a dorky game, but then again, Thor had a dork buried deep inside him. He hadn't always been part of an armed-to-the-teeth, bank robbing squad whose members all took their names from comic book gods.

Odin had binoculars on the bank's second-level offices.

I was watching the street and monitoring the grand entrance.

Saying the Prime Royale was an elegant bank would be the understatement of the year. With its gleaming white marble entrance and soaring columns, it was the Taj Mahal of banks. The entrance was flanked by two palm trees that were so perfectly shaped they looked fake.

In addition to money, the Prime Royale held some of the most priceless jewels in the world. This wouldn't be the biggest prize financially, but it would be the most notorious.

A pair of doormen dressed up in black suits and top hats, stood at the ready to pull the doors open for the fabulous patrons, which added to the fairytale feel of the whole thing.

Inside, the vaults had vibration sensors and the ceilings were fully wired. There were motion detectors in hidden areas. Kick alarm buttons, state-of-the-art laser trips, and more. Real Mission Impossible stuff.

Needless to say, my hunky bank robbers were obsessed with hitting the place.

Zeus was the only one who'd wanted to do it at first, but then Odin and Thor had gotten on board, and when they'd found two rips in the security fabric of the bank, suddenly we had a timetable. It was full steam ahead.

This wouldn't be an old school takeover robbery, my guys' usual specialty; it would be an out-and-out infiltration—another of my guys' specialties.

Odin took a break from his binoculars to give me a look that said he was thinking about another kind of infiltration.

Um...yes please!

I gave him a wicked smile.

He clapped a hand onto my thigh.

My belly tightened.

We didn't usually fool around on stakeout, but then, my guys had never met a rule they didn't want to break.

"You have a count on the west office?" Thor asked.

"Still three," Odin said, raising the binoculars back up and getting back to business.

A stakeout in preparation for a robbery involved counting and timing lots of things.

The hugest security fabric rip was that the Prime Royale was getting a central air upgrade. This meant a portion of the ceiling security was off at any one time due to the upgrade work. The HVAC crew doing the work had recently taken on a hot member with nut-brown hair and a body like a tank.

Zeus.

Just getting him on the crew as a last-minute replacement for the real guy had taken more planning than the storming of Normandy, but it had worked. Naturally, Zeus knew everything about engineering from his time working for a very secret branch of U.S. Intelligence. He was probably giving the Prime excellent value for their maintenance dollar, if you didn't count the fact that we'd be ripping them off.

The other rip was that my guys' criminal friend Matteo had acquired something called the tertiary codes, which he'd gotten off a drug-addicted guard. Between Zeus inside, the ceiling sensor compromise, and Matteo's codes, the opportunity was just too big for them to pass up. It was like one of those once-in-a-lifetime astronomy events.

Of course, there was also the matter of a very weird warning that we'd received. A note from an Abe Lincoln cosplayer telling us not to follow our passions or there'd be trouble. Specifically: *"Passion has helped us, but can do so no more. It will in future be our enemy. Reason, cold, calculating, unimpassioned reason, must furnish all the materials for our future support and defence."*

We still didn't know who had delivered the warning, but it didn't work; in fact, it had the opposite effect, like a flag to a bull, or more like three very growly and sexy bulls. "We need to put reason over passion? They can fuck off!" Zeus had said. "If they have info, then tell us or fuck off, because the Prime is ours."

Sure, it's healthy not to worry what other people think, but I couldn't help but burn with curiosity. What kind of person delivered a note like that? Why in that manner? What was their motive? Did they know something they wanted us to be wary about? Or were they just messing with us?

It was so weird!

"Someday we'll know," Thor had said.

Not hugely helpful.

And we were full steam ahead with the bank. For twelve days we'd been outside in different vehicles. Twelve long, boring days. We all had accounts, and each of us had been inside making deposits.

You got to know a lot about a place in twelve days.

I'd already identified the softest time, security-wise—it was fifteen minutes every day, starting at eleven. That was when the manager went out for bagels. At that point, the guards relaxed. One of them liked to flirt with one of the desk clerks. So far, it had happened each and every day.

I grabbed the iPad from Thor. "My turn for an awareness break."

Instead of taking my turn at my favorite online game, Dazzle Dipper, I had something to show them. A hotel on the Tunisian island of Jerba.

We had made some great scores in the past few months, and I'd insisted on socking away the money in an offshore account. We could retire as is, but if we got half the money they thought we'd get for this job, we could retire in disgusting luxury. And Tunisia doesn't have an extradition treaty, always a plus.

I got to the page and showed it to Odin first.

He gazed at it, all amber eyes under lush, dark lashes, moppy hair, and all of that extreme hotness. The scar over his deeply bronzed right cheekbone moved as he twisted his lips in disapproval.

I was there when he'd gotten that scar—and when he'd refused to let Thor stitch it up.

Poor Odin. He's always looked more like a model than a hardened criminal, much to his own disgust. He'd obviously thought that a big, nasty scar would change all that, but no.

The scar only made him hotter.

"I know Jerba," Odin said. "*Fucking-g* paradisiacal spot." He always pronounced certain g's hard, which made him delightfully easy to mimic.

"That's the idea." I handed the thing to Thor.

"Nice." Thor scrolled through the images.

"They have hot tubs. A hot tub on the balcony overlooking the sea," I said.

"Sure," Thor said. "But we're not the vacationing type."

"It's not for a vacation. It's where we should live."

They both looked at me as if I'd sprung boing-eyes out of my eye sockets.

"We can't live there," Odin said.

"Why not?" I asked.

Thor snorted. "Because."

"Oh, thanks for clearing that up," I said.

"We're visiting vengeance on those who *fucking-g* betrayed us," Odin said.

"Haven't you heard?" I asked. "The best revenge is living well."

Odin rolled his eyes. "The best revenge is for their skin to melt slowly and painfully in the *fucking-g* fire of our wrath."

I didn't have much of a reply to that, so I continued on. "There's a free clinic Thor could volunteer at. You could do your art, Odin. Zeus can amuse himself. I'm sure I could find a way to amuse myself. With you guys."

Thor raised an eyebrow. "Correction. *We* amuse ourselves with *you*."

I gave him a look.

He touched my cheek. "Do you need a demonstration? Of us amusing ourselves with you? Sating ourselves on your body?"

Desire shot down clear through my core. "Be serious." I took the iPad from Thor and shoved it at Odin, who was again peering through the binoculars. "Look at it. Imagine yourself there."

"I know what Jerba looks like." Tunisia wasn't where he was from originally, but surely he was homesick for the Middle East. The call to prayer. The specific kind of heat. The strange pop music. The desert.

"Imagine yourself sitting on that balcony," I said. "We could retire here."

"We don't retire," Odin said.

"Why?" I asked. "Why can't we retire? We have so much money. Like, *so* much."

"We haven't delivered enough pain," Odin said.

"When will we have delivered enough pain?" I asked.

"When ZOX screams like a furry little mongoose. Especially Agent Denko."

Thor's expression turned grim.

I frowned. And not just because I didn't know what a mongoose was. The whole vengeance thing was getting to me.

Their vengeance was righteous, yes, and it was driven by a burning fire, ever since the secret agency they'd devoted their lives to had betrayed them.

Taking down banks, the most public of crimes, was the best *fuck you* two secret agents and a doctor could come up with.

It was something I loved about them at first. But as the weeks had turned into months, I'd become uncomfortable with running on pure vengeance.

I wanted better for them. Because I loved them, even though we'd never said the words to each other.

Loving them was scary, because my beautiful bank robbers were doomed, according to a good number of people.

I usually enjoyed beautiful, doomed things, but the constant threat of losing them?

When would it end?

Chapter Two

"Teller two on her way to a smoke break," Thor said.

I checked my my lucky bank-robbing wig in the mirror—long blonde hair with bangs—ideal for fitting in with the Beverly Hills peeps. In real life, I'd cut my hair short and dyed it platinum blonde. Before that, in my life on the sheep farm, it was long and red.

Satisfied with my wig, I straightened my diamond necklace. One of the good things about casing this place were the extremely fabulous outfits required to look the part. Today I wore a pink silky shirt dress with gold heels.

I sat back and sighed dramatically. "One thing's for sure—living in a vacation paradise would be a hell of a lot more exciting than sitting in this stupid truck doing the most boring thing on the planet."

Odin lowered his binoculars. He had a gleam in his eye that spelled trouble. "This is boring to you, Isis? Do we need to make it un-boring? In a perhaps excruciatingly pleasurable manner?"

"Are you going to tell me you wouldn't rather be lounging in the sun on a tropical island?" I countered.

I had timed my impudence perfectly—I had to be inside the bank in a few minutes. They wouldn't be able to start anything sexy.

Thor looked over at me sadly. He and Odin were dressed in silky shirts and nice slacks, also disguised as patrons of the Prime. They were going in later. "This is boring you, Isis? Oh, no," he said. Thor always acted a little sad when I made an infraction for which I'd have to be erotically punished, though I happened to know he was feeling quite the opposite.

I swallowed, feeling a thrill directly between my legs. "You can't start something. It's almost eleven. I have to make my deposit and check things out." My job was to go in there every day at eleven and make sure things were still soft and observe the different ways in which they were soft.

I knew a lot about banks, having worked at one. These two men—Thor and Odin—along with their leader, Zeus, had taken me away from that life three months back.

As their hostage.

Being held hostage by three hunky bank robbers had turned out to be wonderful in many, many ways.

"We can't start something?" Thor lowered his voice into a sexy rumble. "How is it that we can't start something? Let me ask you—"

"Stop," I laughed, knowing what he'd ask.

He rested a commanding hand on the side of my neck. "Let me ask you who in this vehicle must let us use her body for our pleasure whenever we see fit? Who was that?"

"B-but…" I looked at the bank clock. It was nearly time.

"Who in this vehicle is ours to command?" he continued. "Whatever and wherever we want you?" He placed a hand on my thigh and started moving it up just to demonstrate. "Who?"

"But…"

He moved his hand higher. "We will take you wherever and however we please."

I could feel the wetness between my legs. "We can't do anything until *after* I make the deposit. You have to pay attention to this retirement idea."

Odin grabbed my hair. "Oh, goddess," he whispered. "We're not the ones who started something by complaining."

"Unbutton your top," Thor whispered. "Slowly, the way we like."

"Excuse me?"

Odin let me go and pulled a box from the glove compartment.

"Is Odin going to have to put you over his knee?" Thor asked.

My eyes widened at the box. It looked too small for a paddle.

Thor continued with the questions. "Do I have to unbutton your dress for you? Or will you do it like a good hostage?"

"My deposit," I breathed, pulse pounding.

Thor turned and put a finger under my chin. "Now. Or things might get intense."

With trembling hands, I undid the gold buttons on my pink frock.

"You are so slow, goddess." Odin finished the job, gently undoing the buttons all the way down to my belly button. He pushed aside the fabric to reveal my lacy bra, and ran his warm, heavy hands over my breasts.

I hissed out a breath I didn't know I'd been holding as Thor nibbled my earlobe. "Knit your fingers," he whispered, "and lock them behind your neck. We're almost out of time."

"You guys!"

Thor grabbed my wrists and put them behind my head, holding them there and staring hard into my eyes, pinning me with his gaze. Suddenly I was at the point of no return in terms of control. It's like flying off a ski jump where you abandon yourself to the whims of physics.

Or the whims of men who are dangerous, doomed, and beautiful.

The sense of calm and bliss flowed over me as I knit my fingers.

My breasts became much more prominent when I had my hands behind my neck like that. They rose and fell with each breath.

"Hello," Odin said, stroking my belly, running his hands back up to my bra.

He pulled the lace down off my nipples, which lit up with electricity as he grazed them with the rough pads of his fingers. He tucked the lace under my breasts, plumping them up in the cruelly cool air that flowed out of the air conditioner. My nipples pebbled and my breasts stood at attention, begging to be touched.

He leaned over and put his lips to one and sucked, sending throbs of pleasure clear to my clit.

"Oh." I slid down in the seat, getting into the moment. Vaguely it came to me that Zeus would be angry if I missed making the deposit at eleven.

Some things can't be helped.

Thor untied the belt of my shirt dress. "You're not done undressing yourself," Thor said, unbuttoning the rest of the buttons, all the way down to the hem. He pulled apart two sides of the silky fabric to reveal panties that went with the bra.

"These windows aren't *that* tinted," I said breathlessly, monitoring the face of a passerby.

"You love an audience," Odin said, taking a nipple between his fingers and rolling it, squeezing, then relaxing, then squeezing again.

I exhaled sharply.

It was scary how Odin always knew what I wanted—sometimes even before I did. Like Zeus, Odin had been in the intelligence agency that was now trying to kill us—as a techie and psychological ops guy. When he wasn't figuring out how to outwit our enemies, he was concentrating on driving me mad in sexy ways. His latest discovery was a soft-to-hard-to-soft touch.

I pushed up my pelvis as Thor slid his hand under the elastic of my panties. When he cupped my mound, I exhaled sharply. Then he pushed a finger into the crease between my slick lips.

"Yes," I hissed, undulating under his firm touch.

"Whenever and wherever," Thor whispered, breath hot in my ear, and then he plunged in his tongue, fucking my ear with warm wetness as he invaded my clit with his finger.

"Yes," I said. "Anytime. Whatever you want." I would've said anything at that point. I would've given them anything. I was right on the verge, and they both knew it.

Again, Odin pinched my nipple.

"I'm going to come."

"Don't you dare." Odin softened his movements. "And it's almost eleven."

"Fuck it," I said as the pleasure began to build dangerously high.

"What kind of attitude is that?" Odin asked.

And suddenly his fingers were gone. I opened my eyes when I heard a click.

He held the open box on his lap, angled so that I couldn't see what was inside. I had the feeling it might be something I wouldn't like, though it was hard to do any quality thinking with Thor's tongue thrusting into my ear as he fingered me mercilessly.

Odin stroked a hand over my breast. "Eyes closed," he said.

I closed my eyes and waited, feeling alert and exposed.

Thor laid off me, removing his hand from my panties and his tongue from my ear.

I felt a warm finger touch the underside of my breast, lifting it slightly, and then the bite of something hard closing onto my nipple. Pain sparked through me, arrowing straight down to my clenched pussy as I gasped. Slowly, it transformed into a kind of wild aliveness. And then a wild goodness. And then a wild pleasure.

I began to breathe harder.

I felt a finger under my other breast. A slight lift, preparing the nipple to receive the clamp. I braced for the shot of pain...and then...nothing.

"Eyes remain closed," Odin whispered, knowing I'd want to watch and be ready for the other clamp to go on. "Fingers stay knit."

I swallowed, heart racing, dreading that shot of pain. The longer I waited, the more sensitive the area seemed to become. I could feel the air currents in the car play on the tip of my nipple. Hell, at this point I could feel butterflies flapping their wings in Tanzania on my nipple; that's how keyed up I was.

Waiting.

Needing.

Suddenly craving.

"Please, please," I begged.

His voice was husky. Highly turned on. "Are you ready to feel this *thing-g*, Isis? To receive it gratefully?"

"Yes," I whispered.

Odin waited a beat. Another. And then the bite.

My eyes flew open as I hissed out a breath of air. Was it possible to come from just this?

Odin looked stern. "Did I tell you not to open your eyes?"

Crap. My heart pounded. I looked down at my nipples. Each was adorned with a plastic clamp that had a square bead attached to the end of it. The teeth of the clamps were softer and blunter than I'd imagined from the way they'd felt.

Thor shook his head. "Ignoring an order. And it's still morning."

Odin brought a hand up to caress my cheek. "Over Thor's lap. Now."

"What?" I protested.

"Is that a Mississippi?" Odin asked.

Mississippi was my safe word.

"Bend over Thor's lap, ass in the air. Now."

I swallowed and got up on my knees, there in the front seat.

People were walking up and down the sidewalk, oblivious to the mayhem in our vehicle.

"Bend over. Now," Odin said. "No funny business."

I shifted and bent over his lap, face to Thor's thigh, as Odin had commanded. I reached up with my hands and grabbed onto the driver's side arm rest, ass in air.

The nipple clamps were just heavy enough that their downward pull was strangely pleasurable. Even kind of exciting.

My blood raced. I never knew what Thor and Odin would do.

Thor pulled down my thong to my knees, exposing my ass to the frigid air. He slid his hands over my ass cheeks, softly and gently, creating friction and heat. "This is for your own good, goddess." His hand neared my heated core. I held my breath, desperate for him to touch me there. "Because it is nearly eleven."

"What do you mean? I thought..."

"That you'd be allowed to blow off your mission?" Odin said. "Oh, no. No, no, no."

I tensed up as Thor's fingers neared my clit again, grazing over my swollen lips just briefly before sliding away.

"You're killing me," I gasped.

"That's not what I call it." He moved his hand back, sliding his fingers into my hot folds, sending bolts of pleasure through me.

"Metaphorically," I whispered, letting my forehead drop more deeply into his lap and press against his steely hard cock through his pants, even though that wasn't the game we were playing. I wasn't supposed to be touching them in this game.

"Goddess," he warned, drawing his expert fingers in and out through my juices, slowly, with just enough pressure to drive me wild. He continued, just because he could. Then he found my entrance with the tip of his finger and he invaded my hole.

It was like heaven. He drew it out and pressed in with two fingers.

I pressed back, needing more. Just more. "Yes," I gasped.

"Ten-fifty-eight," Odin said.

I didn't know why they were still thinking I'd go into the bank at this point. The only place I was going right now was a yummy version of down.

"You are so wet for us," Thor whispered.

"Yes. Let's do this," I begged, imagining Thor's fat cock plunging into me. Or I could suck Thor's cock while Odin fucked me, a favorite activity of ours. My ass was feeling needy, stuck up in the cold air.

"Spread your knees," Odin said.

"What?"

"As much as you can."

I complied. I felt Thor withdraw his fingers, slicking my juices over my asshole. He pressed a finger at my puckered opening.

"Uh," I said, feeling the excitement flow through me.

He pushed his fingers a little ways in and then something startling happened: my nipple clamps began to vibrate.

"Oh, my God!" I exclaimed.

I tried to get up, but Thor had fisted my hair, keeping my face firmly pressed into the warm and delicious topography of his lap with his hard cock posing as Mount Everest. My ass waited helplessly for whatever they would decide to do. My body was to be used for their utter pleasure. "Was that a Mississippi?"

"No," I gasped as the nipple clamps vibrated on, sending pulsing, throbbing excitement all through me. "Remote control," I gasped.

Thor pushed his finger deeper into my asshole and the vibrations got stronger.

I panted, feeling melty inside. His finger felt too thick, too huge, but in a decidedly good way. "Enough," I gasped.

"Sorry, goddess," Thor said, pushing deeper. The pleasure was excruciating. I was about to break apart in a million little pieces.

"That is only one part of your punishment," Odin said.

What was he talking about? The clamps stilled, finally, and Thor pulled out his finger.

"Noooo!" My belly felt light. Suspended. Full of butterflies.

Odin narrowed his eyes. "Is that a command?"

I didn't know what anything was at that point, but I knew enough to say no, to simply wait helplessly for whatever would come next.

I didn't have to wait long. I felt a cool drip of something land on the entrance of my asshole. Then another drip, then another. My sex pulsed with every drip and then I felt fingers—Odin's— slicking a rough circle at the tightened entrance of my asshole. The fingers left, replaced with something that felt larger and thicker than Thor's finger.

"What is that?" I whispered. "It's too big."

Thor stroked my hair. "Just relax." He reached around the front of me and stroked between my legs as Odin pressed the impossibly large, bulb-feeling thing into my asshole.

"It feels so huge," I gasped.

"Relax, goddess, it'll be fun," Odin whispered in his husky way. "Take it in."

Little by little, Odin pressed it in, creating a feeling that was at once evil and wonderful.

"Breathe." Thor kept up his stroking, pushing me closer and closer to the edge. Everything in me was turning warm and wanting as Odin pushed the smooth, firm object in deeper and deeper.

I began to enjoy the strange discomfort of being filled up so slowly and hugely. I'd had a cock in there before, but never some- thing smooth and round.

In he pushed. I could feel the thing stretching my asshole, hitting the nerve bundles inside. The strange, delicious feeling of it went into my chest, even into my head, and it seemed to connect with the hard pinch on my nipples. I felt like one of those maps of the night sky with lines connecting stars to make pictures. The little blowjob. Big ménage. Steely cock major. The concubine. Ass- bulb and nipple-clip starburst.

Suddenly the thing was all the way in, and the muscles of my asshole contracted around it, as if of their own volition.

And not only was this large, smooth object in my asshole, but it had a part attached that pressed over my clit, too. Like a bulb in my asshole attached to a thumb that pressed onto the most sensitive part of my anatomy.

"There we go." Thor slapped my ass, then he pulled my thong up over it.

"What are you doing?"

He tugged me up by my hair. "Sit down," he commanded.

"W-what?" I couldn't imagine sitting. The way it would press into me.

"Is this something you can't handle?" Odin asked.

I kind of didn't understand the question. It was a lot of intensity zinging around inside of me.

I twisted and pretended to sit, putting almost no pressure on my ass, and even then, the bulb felt huge in my ass and the lip thing pressed mercilessly onto my clit.

"Sit for real," Thor growled.

A wave of sensation rolled through my belly.

Why were his growly commands so hot? It seemed like it broke all the laws of physics or something.

I let my full weight settle onto the seat, feeling filled up and fucked and controlled, and it wasn't even lunchtime.

"You need to get ready to do your deposit," Odin said.

I looked at him like he'd lost it. "I can't go in there like this!"

"Of course you can." Odin pulled the cups of my bra clear over the nipple clamps, which kicked the pinchy sensation up a notch, and then, calmly and efficiently, he redid the buttons on my dress.

"Are you kidding?" I exclaimed. "I won't be able to concentrate."

"Do you know how they train horses before a race?" Odin asked. He waited, seeming to expect an answer.

I regarded him dimly, not quite understanding why he was asking this. Was I being quizzed on obscure sports trivia now?

"They sometimes train them by running them through knee-deep ocean water. So that when they run on land, where the resistance is gone, they fly. This is your ocean water. We need to know you can focus during all types of situations as part of our gang." Odin's fingers worked quickly. "We need your focus sharp."

I straightened my collar and looked down. Even with the bra over them, you could see the angular outlines of the nipple contraptions through the pink silk.

"Don't worry," Thor said. "It only looks a little obscene. You'll fit right in."

"They're motorized," I said.

Odin gave me a sly look.

"You can't switch them on when I'm in there. And what if the butt thing falls out?"

"It won't. Trust me." Odin gripped my chin and turned my head to him. "And if you come before you get back here, you will not enjoy your punishment."

I wondered what he meant by *not enjoy*. Hanging out with dirty-minded bank robbers, you quickly learn that not enjoy could mean lots of things, and sometimes *not enjoy* involved a whole lot enjoyment.

Still, I didn't want to fail this mission. I wanted them to understand that they could trust me to hold up my end during any operation.

Odin handed me my clutch, which went with my silky shirt dress. Thor got out and held the door open.

My blood raced. I was really going in there like this.

Okay, then.

I stepped onto the sidewalk in my high heels and paused, keenly aware of my nipples and, even more so, of the sensitized bud between my legs. Every time I moved, the area was caressed by the thumb end of the *bulb lodged in my asshole*. It was like an invading presence inside me, turning me on against my will.

"I feel..." I took a step away from the SUV and the thumb rubbed my sex.

"How? How do you feel?" Odin asked.

"Like I'm going to die of horniness," I gasped. "Like I'm going to come at any second."

"You fail before you even start?" Odin said.

"No! No way. But you're not really going to put those nipple things on when I go in there, right?" I asked. "People might see them vibrating. It's not a good way to fit in with the clientele," I added.

Odin grinned. "I will not vibrate the nipple clamps while you are inside."

Well, that was something. I put on my movie star sunglasses.

Odin already had his camera out to record the manager leaving. It was time.

I walked around the front of the shiny black vehicle, stunned at how wickedly the thing between my legs rubbed and caressed my sensitive folds.

I swallowed. *Focus,* I commanded myself. *It's just feeling. You can do it.*

I had to do it.

Chapter Three

I FORCED MY MIND ONTO THE DETAILS OF THE BANK AS I mounted the hard, gleaming front steps. The smiling doormen opened the doors for me. Did their smiles seem too smiley?

No. No way could they know, I told myself.

I walked in and clicked into professional mode, letting my awareness spread across the floor. I counted the employees and noted their positions.

Odin had snuck a few tiny cameras in there and mounted them on architectural detailing, but nothing was quite as effective as actually being there, where you could feel the place, become part of its ecosystem.

And being that I'd worked at a bank, I picked up things other people didn't.

We'd all been happy when we'd figured out that the manager of the Prime Royale, a fit and well-tanned blond man of maybe forty-five, was an asshole. Asshole managers created a pressurized situation while they were present, which meant a release of pressure when they left.

We'd be robbing the bank after hours later in the week, but a day or two before the robbery, Zeus would have to go into the lobby and get at the environmental control panel. We were planning to handle that part of the operation during this lax late-morning time, helped along by a bit of a diversion.

The manager leaned on the customer side of the teller window —giving some last instructions before his break, I guessed. I got into the line at the very next window and listened. Something about bundling ones. He liked to make sure the tellers didn't slack off while he was gone. Which of course meant the opposite. Such is the way of asshole bosses and their employees.

One of the men at a desk discreetly pulled his smartphone out of his pocket and lowered it into his lap. He'd start texting as soon as the big guy was out.

Still, even with all of our expertise and current advantages, the Prime Royale would be hard to rob. We had a new partner on board because of it—Matteo. Matteo was a tough, tattooed dude who once ran with a girl gang known as the Giraffes, though most people called them the Gigis.

Matteo had been robot dancing at a club frequented by the criminal underworld of LA when I first saw him. And let me assure you, robot dancing in no way lessened his toughness. In fact, I can safely say that robot dancing with a machine gun slung over your back tends to add to your toughness factor. It says to the world that you can do whatever weird-ass thing you want, and you just don't care.

Normally, my guys would've never pulled Matteo into a job, but he had those codes to the tertiary alarm system. The Prime Royale was full of jewels, and Matteo planned to use his cut of the jewels to bribe his way back into the good graces of the Gigis. They'd let him be a member once upon a time when he was with Macy. I doubted they'd ever let him back in—they seemed pretty committed to being a girl gang—but who knows, maybe Macy would forgive him.

I was second in line now. I stood to the side, where I wouldn't show up on the front-and-center bank camera, feeling proud of how much I was observing and how normal I was acting in spite of being on the verge of an orgasm.

I watched the way all the employees watched the blond manager. He was pretty good looking, but you could tell he thought he was extremely good looking.

I glanced away as he passed. I didn't need to catch this guy's eye.

And that's when the unit stuck up my ass and between my legs began to vibrate. Softly, gently. It wasn't just a fancy dildo. It was some sort of clit-and-butt vibrator. A clit-and-butt-erator.

I sucked in a silent breath.

Because, oh, *wow*, it felt so good. I bit my lip and focused through the pleasure. I'd show my guys how well I could concentrate.

So I stood there, working to regain mental control over the intensity of the feeling, which was not easy; the pulsing clit-and-butt-erator pressure coupled with the relentless squeeze of the nipple clamps was quite delicious. I thought about what Zeus often told me—*keep a wide, calm focus.* He'd typically say it when we were casing a place or doing something risky, but I felt it could apply to this situation. *Don't work at it, let the environment come to you.*

I took a breath and relaxed, letting my focus go wide, just giving in to the sensation and the surroundings, and I suddenly got what he meant; I felt observant at a new level. Crystal-sharp, even.

Like I could do anything.

It was my turn. I took on a confident, casual attitude. Just as I approached the window, the vibrations stopped. They were watching the feed, of course, and I felt a bit annoyed—I could've done the deed buzzing. I greeted the teller and began my transaction. Standing at the teller window gave me a good view of the back of the house. This was a tight operation, and even though my guys were talented robbers who'd been trained to work undercover in enemy territory and fight covert wars, too, I worried about this job. This was the mythical *Big One*.

We could retire on it—that was my secret idea.

My guys rarely thought about the future, but I hoped that I was changing that. At least they'd stopped blowing one hundred percent of their money on fancy hotels and champagne and other wasteful lavishness. It was more like sixty percent now.

The teller, a pretty woman with jet-black bangs, counted out a small pile of twenties. I took them, thanking her, and nestled them carefully into my wallet.

Five minutes later, the smiling, top-hatted doormen simultaneously opened the golden doors of the Prime Royale for me and I strolled out, stepping down the marble stairs between the suspiciously perfect palms, feeling pretty damn pleased with myself.

As soon as I hit the sidewalk, the vibrations started—the nipple clamps and the unit between my legs—both at once. It was an intense hit of pleasure. I wanted so badly to come, and briefly I considered stopping at the bus stop bench and just letting it happen. I was out of the bank now; the test was over. But I strolled on down to our stakeout SUV. Because I was in control!

When I got to the sidewalk side, I could see tough-ass Matteo in the front seat with Odin, talking animatedly.

Crap.

I'd die if he knew I had little vibrating implements all over me. The back door cracked open. Thor. He slid over and I got in with the stuff still vibrating.

"Him Matteo," I said in a surprisingly relaxed tone.

"Hey, Ice." He twisted around in the seat. "How's it look in there?"

"Same as yesterday," I said, proud to manage a semi-normal voice. "Relaxed. The plainclothes who guards the side is struggling with bad allergies right now, too, and he's very unaware. I hope they don't improve for a while. Not to be a bitch."

Thor snorted.

"I'm liking that," Matteo said. "Liking it." He had brown hair and a wide face and lots of tattoos on his arms, and he was very much a guy's guy.

His eyes fell to my breasts. I couldn't blame him—it looked like I was wearing some very serious nipple jewelry. I quickly began to dig inside my bag in a way that obscured them, hoping he hadn't noticed the vibrations, because let's face it, that would look really unprofessional.

Odin asked him about some small aspect of timing, and Matteo turned back.

I smiled. Did my crafty bank robber not like Matteo looking at my breasts? Yeah, maybe he should have thought about that before he put *vibrating clamp contraptions on them.*

The vibrations ceased, and I relaxed just a bit.

I was hoping Matteo would leave after he answered the question—he was stationed in the park today—but he rambled on. He had extensive opinions about pretty much everything; the man was just as brilliant as my guys, but very opinionated.

The plan was that Zeus would stay behind in the ducts after the bank closed on the day of the robbery and let the three guys in. I had the big outside support role. It was a large and complicated operation.

"We're gonna get hungry in there," Matteo said. "Two words: beef jerky."

"That shit's full of nitrates," Thor said.

"Don't worry, doc. Not the place I get it from," Matteo said. "All natural."

I smiled. Opinionated Matteo knew where to get the best of everything. I could see the Gigis getting pissed at him and kicking him out. But he had a good heart, too.

Odin caught my eye as he and Matteo went over the list of tools Zeus was bringing in to conceal in the workspace—one or two a day.

I stiffened, hoping he didn't get it in his head to start up the vibrations. I finally felt normal, or at least I was out of the I-have-to-come-right-now-or-I'll-die zone.

Odin smiled.

I narrowed my eyes and shook my head.

They continued their discussion.

"What is it, goddess?" Thor asked. I didn't have to look at him to see he was grinning.

"Nothing," I said, leaning back.

Surely they didn't want Matteo to know. Matteo would want things professional.

While Zeus mainly liked the idea of robbing the Prime Royale because it was the biggest *fuck you* possible, just one rung below hitting Fort Knox, Matteo wanted a specific set of diamond jewelry, known as the Liz Taylor diamonds, to give to the Gigis.

Odin had originally wanted the Liz Taylor diamonds, too. He'd wanted to wear them to taunt the Gigis because they'd pissed him off on a certain occasion, but the guys made a deal with Matteo in order to get the intel that he had.

It had been agreed that Odin would wear the Princess Harrod sapphires to taunt the Gigis in retaliation for trying to get me to join their gang. Then, after a set amount of time, Matteo would be free to give them the Liz Taylor diamonds, which Odin would not be permitted to wear as a taunt.

I was to get a diamond tiara that was worth more than all of those other jewels put together.

Thor just wanted the money. He'd been crossing the border into Mexico recently to volunteer at a free clinic just south of Tijuana, and they needed equipment badly. He wasn't able to work as a doctor in the States, but he wasn't being bothered so far in Mexico. It was risky as hell, him crossing the border, but being a doctor was important to him. It kept him balanced.

Anyway, everything in our lives was risky as hell. We didn't need a freak warning from a fake Abe Lincoln to know that.

I looked out the window at the beautifully dressed people leading their normal lives, climbing in and out of sleek cars.

Maybe I looked bored, because right then I felt the clamps on my nipples begin to vibrate softly.

It was a surprise at first—so unexpected, so out of my control.

I looked down, sure you would be able to see them going, but they looked the same as before...like I was wearing chunky nipple jewelry.

Only now, that nipple jewelry was sending waves of pleasure clear into the pit of my belly.

I stiffened and glanced at Odin in the front seat. He was messing around on his phone, continuing to go over logistics with Matteo. Of course he'd have made an app for his little contraption.

"What?" Thor asked quietly.

It was then that the pulsing on my clit started.

I turned to him, shifting my legs, closing them together. That only intensified the good feeling.

Thor only had to take one look at my face to get it. "Did I ever tell you how hot you look in that outfit?"

"Thank you," I rasped.

Desire built in my belly. Dimly, I tried to remember why I shouldn't have an orgasm with Matteo in the car.

Thor looked at me warningly and clamped a hand down on my knee. He shook his head, pulled at my leg.

Reluctantly, I parted my legs, which lessened the intensity, but only slightly.

"This is going to go like clockwork," Matteo said from up front.

"Good things come to those who wait," Thor said.

"*Fucking-g* right about that," Odin agreed with a sly glance at me. He'd grown up in Morocco, except for some years in Egypt and an Algerian prison, but I didn't know much more than that. He was very private about his history. "The best things come to those who wait."

Okay, I got the game. If I held out, things would be good.

"Going in too hasty would be such a mistake," Thor said.

"Abso-fucking-*lutely*," Matteo said. "It's all in the planning. It's in knowing how to take advantage of the luck that you spot."

The pleasure of the vibrations was incredibly intense. This thing between my legs was absolutely diabolical. The thumb part pressed perfectly at my clit.

Damn! I lifted my pelvis slightly off the seat, which made the vibrations seem less intense. But it also changed the spot, which made things newly pleasurable. And the leg muscles I was now using wouldn't support me long.

I could see the steely outline of Thor's cock beneath his slacks. I wished I could grab his cock and give him a taste of his own medicine.

Up front, Matteo was talking sound absorbers. He had a special lunchbox for Zeus.

I tried to follow along. Every day Zeus came out to eat his lunch in the park, and one of us switched lunch boxes with him. The new lunchbox would contain a new piece of equipment to smuggle into the bank.

"You're the one meeting him in the park today?" I asked Matteo hopefully.

He looked at his watch. "Fifteen minutes."

Crap! My legs gave out and I had to sit back down again.

The vibrations seemed to redouble, creating an electric feeling that flowed all over my skin.

Oh, my resolve really was weakening. I tried to concentrate on the danger of the job. How frightened I was for my guys.

It helped...marginally.

Thor and Odin were going to be in so much trouble after this.

"I should leave to pick up his sandwich now, though," Matteo said. "Does he want turkey again?"

"Yes, but it won't take fifteen minutes to get his sandwich," Odin said wickedly.

I rested my head back against the headrest and looked out the window. I was going for a look that could be described as *bored*...as opposed to, say, wildly-turned-on sex partner to hot bank robbers.

"We're done here, though," Matteo said. "You guys good?"

"I'm good," I said.

Matteo looked at me funny. Maybe it was my tone. "You two need to have a backup vehicle stashed," he said.

"We're already on it," Thor said, hand still on my leg. "We'll have two of them." He squeezed my thigh. Excitement winged through me.

Matteo leveled a glance at me. "You're good to drive if it comes to that?" Drive, in that sentence, meant worlds more than simply operating a motor vehicle. It meant, did I have the guts and focus to do it?

"She's more than good to drive," Odin said. "Ice is one of the best."

One of the best. I smiled. "I'm ready for anything." And just then, I was good with being extensively pleasured without release.

"Okay." Matteo pushed on his sunglasses. Finally! Then he turned back. "How many banks have you all hit this year?"

Oh, my God.

Odin frowned, thinking.

Nooo! I slid down in my seat.

"Calendar year or since last September?" Thor asked lazily.

"Jesus," Matteo said. "Since last September. Whatever."

"A lot," I said.

"How many is that?" he asked.

Odin and Thor exchanged glances.

Pick a number, any number, I thought as the intensity built.

"Fifteen," Thor finally said.

"Hmm," Odin said. "I was going to go a dozen, but we average more than one a month, I guess. So, yeah, about fifteen."

Matteo snorted. "You don't even count. You guys work too hard."

"That's what I've been telling them," I said. "They need relief. They really do."

"A few hours a month? That's too hard?" Thor said.

"You know what I mean," Matteo said.

"Vengeance never sleeps," Odin said.

"Yeah..." Matteo inched open the door, "but maybe vengeance deserves to chill sometimes."

"Those motherfuckers *wish* we were dead," Thor said.

"Okay." Matteo finally got out.

I swallowed, trying to keep my eyes steady on the seam of the seat back, trying not to pant. It didn't help that the vibrations on my nipples and my clit had changed in character to a soft pulsing.

"Well then..." Matteo seemed like he was about to close the door. Leaving.

Then he leaned back in. "Did you guys get that on your tattoo yet?"

"We've started it," Odin said. "You WISH we were dead, motherfuckers. On a scroll that an angel holds." Way earlier, we'd gotten a cloud with four lightning bolts, symbolizing the four of us, on our ankles. We'd meant to do the 'Motherfuckers' one above the original tattoo, but we'd decided it would be better on the biceps due to the hairiness of Zeus's calves.

"We were thinking of having it partly in Latin," Thor added. "But then who the fuck could read it?"

Matteo chuckled.

Odin had already started on the addition to our tattoos. I liked the idea of that tattoo at first, but lately, I wondered if it was the best tattoo for us.

You WISH we were dead, motherfuckers.

Who gets a motto tattooed on their skin about how much their enemies hate them and wish they were dead? It seemed negative—even a little dangerous on a new-age/positive visualization level—to put such a wish on your skin.

This thought damped my libido enough for me to pay attention to the conversation again.

"Isis has the tattoo that is furthest along. I already did her angel and part of the scrollwork. You want to see it?" Odin asked him suddenly.

I swallowed. *Say no. Go!* I pleaded in my mind, wishing I could blast my thoughts right into Matteo's brain. *Go! Go!*

"You guys..." Matteo shook his head. "I'll see them when they're done."

"I want you to see it," Odin said. "I insist. Isis." He put down the armrest between the front seats and patted it, then gazed back at me, evil eyes glittering. "Come on. Show Matteo."

I slid forward and displayed my arm. Even that much shifting intensified the vibrations wildly. Odin pulled me forward further so that my arm was under the slash of sunshine on the seat. I could feel the waves building in the pit of my stomach. Nearing lift-off.

"Nice," Matteo said. "Okay, gotta get on this here." He finally got all the way out and shut the door. We watched him walk off.

The vibrations ceased.

I hissed out a breath and flopped back into my seat. "You are both pure evil."

Thor turned to me and began to unbutton my shirt. "You have been a very patient goddess."

"The evilest of evil."

"You know that's not true," Thor said. "Come here." He shifted sideways in the backseat and pulled me up against his chest. His cock was like concrete at the small of my back. I snuggled into it, just to tease him. "But there *was* that matter of backtalk earlier," he whispered in my ear.

Odin got out the driver's side door and shut it. The next thing I knew, he was opening the back door. A shaft of sunlight and heat fell across my bare torso.

I whipped my dress over myself.

He gave me a smug look and got in, closing the door behind him. "As if you don't like an audience."

"Not all the time," I said.

"And not Matteo," Odin said, pulling off my panties.

"I have been so good," I said.

Thor ran his hand over my belly. "I'm going to undo these clips," he whispered. "Are you ready?"

"Please," I mumbled. "Anything."

He reached around to my front and unclamped one. I gasped at the release of it. Odin leaned in and licked it lightly, melting me with sensation.

"It's too much! Lighter." My nipples were always so wildly sensitive after being clipped, which was both good and bad.

Odin lightened his licking. I reached up under him and grabbed his cock, winding my legs partly around him.

"Goddess," he breathed, blowing on my nipple as Thor released the clip from the other one. "Turn over," he said.

I complied, moving to my hands and knees, which put me face to face with Thor.

Thor grabbed my hair and took my mouth in a hard kiss while Odin ran his hands over my butt cheeks.

I felt his fingers move down my thighs, spreading tiny shivers, making the sound of skin on skin in the quiet car. Then he slid his hands up again. I felt when he grasped the clit-and-butt-erator. Gently, he worked it out, pulling the bulbous portion from my asshole.

The feeling of emptiness was immediately followed by a stinging slap.

I gasped. "What was that for?"

"Unprofessionalism." He slapped my ass again. I felt the pain and pleasure of it pulse through me.

"*I* was unprofessional?" I protested. "I was as professional as James Bond in there. I was the very picture of professional."

"Not when you wanted to blow off your 11:00 a.m. deposit."

He slapped me again, and it stung hot and icy, then he set his warm hand on the sting, and I felt his warm lips touch it. I wanted him like a fever. I loved these guys, and I wanted them both in me. Odin spoke, finally. His growl grabbed my belly. "Turn around."

I turned back around to find him pulling his pants off, his cock at attention. My pulse raced wildly.

"Hold her legs apart, Thor."

From behind me, Thor grabbed the backs of my knees and pulled up, pulling my knees clear to my shoulders.

I leaned my head back on his shoulder, feeling wild with need.

I gasped as Odin stroked his thick, brown cock, hardening himself even more. A warning. A promise. We didn't have to wear condoms anymore—we'd all been tested, and we were monogamous now.

He touched my clit. "Are you wet for me, goddess?" He began to stroke me gently with his thumb.

"Yes. I can't take any more waiting," I gasped.

"You'll take whatever we give you, goddess," Odin whispered tenderly. "Whatever we please, because you are so *fucking-g* beautiful." He came to me then, kneeling between my legs, stroking me, getting me even more on the verge. I looked into his gorgeous eyes, rimmed with those thick lashes, and in my mind, I gave myself over to him completely—my body, my pleasure, my everything. "So *fucking-g* beautiful," he whispered again. He held me with a mischievous gaze as he licked a finger and then touched it to one of my ultra-tender nipples.

"Please," I begged, because I was about to spin out of control.

"Thor," Odin said.

Thor pulled my legs wider. Odin pressed the meaty tip of his cock into my hole. "Is this what you want, goddess?"

"More," I gasped.

He was maybe an inch in, but just that inch felt impossibly thick and good inside me. Then he braced one muscular arm on the front seat headrest and the other on the top of the back seat, caging me and Thor. "Goddess," he said, leaning in for a kiss as he entered me slowly, filling me deliciously.

"Yes." I reached out to him, holding him, pulling him.

He pulled out halfway and thrust in again.

"Yes," I gasped, all out of meaningful things to say.

Thor let my knees go. I wrapped my legs around Odin as Thor shifted behind me, and I could tell he was doing himself. My guys loved when I came almost as much as I loved it. With his other hand, he reached around me and fingered a nipple.

"Come for me, goddess," Odin said.

But I was already there—maybe that's why he said it, because he knew, and had taken pity on me.

None of it mattered because I dissolved into a million pieces as Odin fucked me and kissed me.

I was a kaleidoscope of sensation.

Odin's fucking movements were becoming primitive, like he was being controlled by something deep and ancient.

Thor panted in my ear.

They were both about to come, the ultimate testosterone sandwich.

"Do me," I said, which was sort of a joke, considering they could hardly do me any more than they were already. But they were both coming. Out of reception range. "Yes," I whispered, stroking Odin's back.

Afterwards, we all collapsed on each other in the back seat, dazed.

"Man," Thor said, caressing my thigh. "When Matteo wouldn't leave and you were on the edge like that, Isis, I thought I might lose it, too."

"That was an evil game," I said.

"But so much fun," Thor said.

Chapter Four

WE HEADED BACK TO MY GUYS' PLACE, A MOD HIDEOUT hidden in the hills. We needed to clean up and change and get back to the bank. It was Matteo's shift to sit on the bank.

Odin took the souped-up Navigator up the steep drive and parked it next to the souped-up Camaro and the souped-up Jetta. My bank robbers liked a shitload of horsepower, if you know what I mean. He engaged the emergency brake and the three of us hopped out.

Odin was the first to spot the package on the stoop. "What the hell is that?" he said, stretching out an arm to the side as if to say *no further.*

We all just stood there, some twenty feet away, staring at the package.

It was definitely weird for there to be a package waiting for us. The mailbox was way down at the end of the drive, and we only ever got junk mail anyway. Not like any of us would ever whip out a credit card and order something online, and all of our bank accounts were offshore, if not offshore of offshore. The only people who knew where we crashed were our closest comrades. And they would know not to leave a package.

Thor squinted at it, eyes brilliant blue in the sunshine. "There is no way this is good," he said.

It was about the size of a shoebox and wrapped in white paper.

"Get back behind the Nav," Odin commanded. We all went back behind the SUV. Odin grabbed a stone and threw it at the package with impressive accuracy. *Bop.* The package rolled and slid.

"Bomb test?" I asked.

Thor, not to be outdone, threw his own damn rock. Thor's rock was larger and he threw it harder. The package rolled.

I gasped.

There was one word written on it in huge, childish block letters: Isis.

It wasn't the cute kind of block letters, either. More like scary-dude-in-a-basement-bent-on-vengeance kind of lettering.

Trust me, crazed-dude-in-a-basement-bent-on-vengeance is not a font you ever want to see your name written in.

"Ice?" Odin asked. "Any ideas...?"

"None."

"What the hell," Thor muttered under his breath. He'd already pulled out his silver Sig. Were they going to shoot it, now?

"Written with the left hand," Odin observed. "To make the writing untraceable. I need gloves."

Thor yanked open the door and pulled what looked like a tissue box from the glove compartment, except it was full of latex gloves. He handed a pair to Odin.

Odin snapped them on. "Stay there."

I held my breath as he headed around and up to the stoop. He picked up the box and held it, simply contemplating it, one hand on either side, like a basketball player about to make a free-throw. Then he lifted it and sniffed it. After that, he put it to his ear and listened, and turned it to examine the paper wrapper folds on one end. For his final act, he licked those folds.

"Yuck," I said.

Thor put a quieting hand on my arm. Odin just stood there,

brows drawn low in a scowl at the package, as if, having exhausted all five senses, he now hoped to receive an ESP communication from it, a feat that wouldn't entirely shock me, I suppose. Odin was the most brilliant of us—a kind of artist who sailed through the highest stratospheres of techie-ness and psychological understanding.

I held my breath as he shook it. Then he turned to us. "I'm *going-g* to open this fucker up. You mind?"

"Go for it," I said.

"Do it," Thor said, strolling up.

"No, stay back." Odin said.

"You better be downwind," Thor grumbled.

"I am." Odin set it back down on the stoop and undid the white paper, careful not to rip anything, pulling it off in a large piece. One of the sides was kind of shiny.

It turns out it was the size of a shoebox because it was a shoebox, with the Nike swoosh on the side. Somehow I doubted it contained shoes. I held my breath as Odin flipped off the lid and bent over the contents.

"What is it?" Thor asked.

"Come see," Odin said.

We went up and stood with Odin, the three of us peering into the box, which contained a plastic baggie with a feather and some gloppy, partly dried, dark reddish-brownish fluid inside of it.

Not shoes, then.

The feather had once been white, but was now half-stained with the fluid, which, let's face it, looked an awful lot like blood. Some of the fluid clung to the sides of the baggie.

"Not really my style. I mean, what ever would I wear them with?" I said, going for the joke, like that might make this less alarming.

My guys weren't amused. Odin carefully unfolded the note. It read, "YOU ARE MINE." In that same blocky, childish lettering.

Okay, now I was scared.

"Do you think this is related to the Abe Lincoln warning?" Thor asked.

"All I know is that I'm *fucking-g* going to kill somebody," Odin said, yanking out his gun. "You stay here with Ice and keep a good eye on the surroundings. I'm taking a walk around, then inside."

"Got it," Thor said, weapon at the ready.

"Then we'll print it, though I don't imagine we'll find much," Odin grumbled. "I can think of a dozen people who know we're here, and none of them would be stupid enough to leave prints."

"Nobody we know is stupid enough to do this in the first place," Thor said. "Maybe somebody is off the rails."

"Maybe." Odin headed off to the side to make a check of the area around the house.

"Oh, my God," I said, heart pounding. Just the writing was so bizarre. And the blood.

"Pig's blood, I bet," Thor said. "Because this paper, it's butcher paper."

"It's *blood*."

Thor looped his arm around my shoulder. "We'll keep you safe, Isis. Nothing and nobody comes between us. Ever. Got it? You know that, right?"

"Yeah, I know," I said, though I couldn't stop shaking. In all the mayhem that was our life now, the one place I'd felt secure was this hideout.

He pulled me tighter. "This shit does not stand."

After a few minutes, Odin came out the front door with a handful of large plastic Ziploc baggies. "Nobody's here." He and Thor bagged the stuff separately and we went in.

"It could be worse. It could be your real name," Thor said once we were safe inside.

That freaked me out even more. If anyone knew my real name, it meant that they could get to my sisters. They thought I was dead, though I sent them money by buying up the wildly overpriced "Paris Hilton" model of sheep wool comforter. It's possible they suspected it was from me, but that's as much as I could do.

He set the package on the kitchen table next to what looked like a tackle box, except it was full of brushes and tiny bottles. A fingerprint kit. Thor pulled on a pair of latex gloves and spread out the paper.

"We have a fingerprint kit?" As soon as I said it, I realized it was a stupid thing to be surprised by. I knew Odin and Zeus as bank robbers and thought of them that way, but they'd come out of intelligence. Spies.

They'd been super cops once.

"You'd be surprised how handy something like this is," Thor said. "Though the last time Zeus used it, it was to find out who pissed in the bird bath during a poker night."

"Zeus was mad as hell," Odin said.

"I'd think that was more the realm of a DNA test," I said, watching Odin brush powder off the butcher paper.

"There's a pole next to the birdbath," Thor explained. "People were drunk. He figured whoever it was would've held onto it for support. And he was right. He made the guy come out and scrub it."

"But, to run fingerprints you need a database of fingerprints," I said.

"There are a few federal databases we can still get into," Odin said.

I nodded. *Right*. They still had a friend or two deep inside the web of government agencies.

"And most of the people we know happen to be in that database, which is convenient at times like these," Odin added.

"We can't tell Zeus about this until he's home with us," Thor said. "He'll go ballistic. No good to have him finding out while he's inside those HVAC ducts."

"Fuck," Odin said, emphatically.

Thor examined the shoebox. "No price tag anywhere. This is a pretty common style, I think. But let me check it out." He grabbed his iPad from his pack.

"No prints on the baggie," Odin said. He opened it up and pulled out the bloody feather with tweezers and set it into a smaller baggie, sealing it up. "Get online, Isis, and see if you can determine the type of bird this comes from."

"How do I do that?" I asked.

"Figure it out," Odin barked. "I'd think if a person is able to find entire cartoon porn websites devoted to fetishes about being taken captive and forcibly ravished by woodsmen, then you could identify a simple feather, right?"

I snatched the baggie. They weren't supposed to tease me about my taste in cartoon porn anymore. Being taken prisoner while walking in the forest and ravished by hunky hooded woodsmen in tights wasn't a fun thought now, in light of this horrible package. If there were no fingerprints, how were they supposed to figure out who sent the box?

"Who cares what bird it's from?" I asked.

"It all matters," Odin said.

"Are you sure you're not just trying to give me something to do so I'm not freaking out?"

"This is an investigation. We glean all the information we possibly can, and then and only then do we assess whether it is worthwhile to know," Odin said.

I sat down at the far end of the table with my laptop and started on my task, trying not to focus too hard on the horror of the darkened blood marring the white feather. Or that somebody would send that to me. I looked up ornithology sites.

It turned out that feathers looked similar from one bird to another, but there were differences. The little feathery strands were called barbs and they had really tiny parts coming off of them called barbules, which is how the barbs stuck together. It was lucky the thing was only half-coated in dried blood.

"Can I borrow the magnifying glass?" I looked up to see Odin using it. "After you're done?" I added.

"Have it now, goddess." Odin came around and set it next to the keyboard. Then he leaned in to kiss my hair. "Whoever did this," he whispered into my hair, "we will run him down to the ends of hell and pull his guts from his belly like fishing rope. Because nobody *fucking-g* threatens you."

Shivers came over me. "Thank you, baby," I whispered, loving him so much. I felt so wonderfully loved and held and protected by these men. My family.

Odin went to a drawer and pulled out a leather case that contained another magnifying glass.

I went back to studying diagrams. I had a feeling we were looking at a pigeon feather, but I hadn't found an exact match. Odin and Thor were discussing everybody who knew where this particular hideout was, who had also met me, creating a list of suspects. They ruled a few people out, like Matteo, who had been with us all day.

Thor set down the iPad. "So apparently every athletic store and discount store in the known world carries this model."

Odin turned the shoebox all around, blowing gently on the dust. "Fucker's full of prints."

"Could be from the shoe store."

Odin set it on the plastic and grabbed a magnifying glass. He examined the top of the box, then dusted the rest of it. "Four different individuals at least. It looks like somebody tried to wipe them—poorly. Good." He took out his smartphone and made a few scans, then hit some keys, sending them, presumably, to their guy in intelligence.

"How long?" I asked.

"We'll see," Odin said. "Our guy can't be obvious about it. He has to put them in a batch already running."

Odin got on the phone with Matteo and asked him to sit on the bank a little longer, explaining the situation and asking if

Matteo had fielded any questions about Isis. He nodded, grunted, and hung up.

I will confess that I was a little bit wary of robbing the Prime Royale with this new development. Especially in light of the last note we got.

"What'd he say?" Thor asked.

"That a shitload of people ask about Isis," Odin said. "They all knew Venus. They're curious."

I looked down at my screen. Venus had been with my guys a few years back. She'd hated being trapped on the run. She'd nearly gotten them caught on a job, and then she killed herself by jumping a hundred feet into a quarry pit. Venus was a tender spot —they spent years blaming and hating themselves for her suicide. Zeus especially blamed himself.

I wondered about Venus often—what she was like, how she interacted with the guys. Times when I felt insecure, I wondered if I really measured up to her. But mostly I felt sad for her, and I thought I would've liked to have known her.

"And our gang cloud tattoo." He pointed his eyes down at my ankle. "Matteo thinks it made you a bigger target. And now the cherub angels on our arms?"

"Hmm," Thor said.

"I love the tattoo. Screw that." At least, I liked the tattoo of an angry cloud with four badass lightning bolts representing the four of us. It showed we were a family, and I was proud to have it.

"You making progress with that feather?" Odin asked.

"A little." I got back to examining the barbules.

Later, Odin sent Thor out to a lab downtown with some of the blood for a DNA test. I knew the place—it was mostly for drug testing and paternity testing, but apparently they could test blood to see what sort of animal it came from.

After that, Odin called Robert Manning, the A/V guy who'd installed surveillance around the driveway and neighborhood and requested extra security cameras installed around the perimeter of the house, so that no inch of tundra would go unfilmed. Then he made sandwiches.

"Thanks," I said as he set down a plate.

"Zeus is *going-g* to freak the fuck out," Odin said.

I nodded glumly, staring at my sandwich. I didn't have much of an appetite, but Odin ate ravenously. It took a lot to make my guys lose their appetites.

"This man will bitterly regret the day he ever so much as thought of you with anything but the purest of admiration."

"I don't want him to think of me at all."

Odin lowered his voice. "Soon he won't."

I got up and washed my hands in the kitchen sink, which looked out over the cozy living spaces of the hideout, decorated in a style I'd describe as mod cabin, built for comfort and relaxation, and not at all flashy. The style involved plush rugs, blocky uphol- stered furniture, and old snowshoes on the wall in front of the fireplace.

Odin eyed me carefully as I sat back down across from him. "You okay?"

I tore off a crusty bit of bread. "It's just creepy. And if it's the same person who sent us that Abe Lincoln warning? Does that make it better or worse?"

"Why warn us of something and then threaten us?" Thor said. "None of it makes sense."

"Hey." Odin came around and settled a hand lightly onto my hair. "We have you, goddess."

"I know, and it's not that I don't think you'll get him, but that doesn't take away the yuckiness of a gift like that."

"We'll hurt him extra for the yuckiness."

I smiled up at him. Odin's lovely Mediterranean skin had bronzed in the LA sun, and he had a perfect five o'clock shadow below his hot, jaggedly scarred cheekbone. "More than pulling his guts from his belly like fishing rope?"

"I'll do it slowly," he growled.

"Oh," I said. Because, what else do you say to that?

"Finish your lunch. We go to the butchers."

Chapter Five

AFTER VISITING EIGHT BUTCHER SHOPS, WE LEARNED one big thing: there are lots of people in Los Angeles buying blood. Some buy sheep and cow blood, but mostly pig's blood. And butchers are happy to supply it; even the supermarket butchers sold it. Some of them chalked it up to the vampire craze. Others sold it for theatrical realism or religious ceremonies.

You never saw it in the case. I suppose that might be a bit much, containers of blood displayed next to the roast beef or sliced ham. *Pig's blood! Try it for your next black magic ritual or Civil War reenactment! Only $9.99 a quart!*

Another thing we learned: they all had the same butcher paper supplier.

I slid into the warm and toasty SUV after the last butcher visit and clicked on my seatbelt. Odin started the engine. "Who the fuck knew about all this?"

"I thought *we* were weird," I said.

"This is not a profitable avenue," he said.

It was nearly four when we got back home. Thor was outside standing next to a ladder over the front door. Up on the top was Robert Manning, the A/V security guy, a tank-like forty-something man with military tattoos all over his arms. He was a former Navy SEAL with blond hair that was always perfectly combed, just long enough to feather back, and it seemed to float around his head in close orbit, as feathered hair sometimes does.

"Just installed one of these in the home of a big star. Can't tell ya who," Manning said.

Well, that star was smart. Hiring the guy who installed video monitoring systems and security gate controls for criminals seemed like a good way to go.

Apparently the gates Manning installed were guaranteed to hold up against any vehicle up to a Humvee. *You got two Hummers, that's where the gate goes*, he'd said to us when we moved back in here. My guys liked him. Manning didn't know who they'd been in their other life, and they'd never worked together, but the four of them had a certain camaraderie, a certain understanding that seemed to go beyond the usual fellow criminal bonds. I always thought they smelled military training on each other.

He stepped down from his ladder, wiping his hands on a rag. "Come on inside, I'll show you the range."

We followed him into the kitchen. He opened a laptop, punched up a website, and entered a code. "I'll be sending all this to you. Here's your number one camera, out front. Number two is in back, and three and four are east and west. Here are the corners. The system stores three days before it records over. Video files are large." He looked up, furrowed brow. "Sorry to hear about all this, miss."

I smiled and nodded. Manning always called me *miss*, and I didn't much like it. It seemed weird and distancing. In general, I didn't entirely like Manning, but it could be because I felt he didn't like me, what with all the distancing *miss* stuff. He was one of those guys who didn't really take women seriously. There were a lot of guys like that in the criminal crowd.

"Be sorry for the one who left that package," Odin said. "They are already dead. They are already *crying-g*."

Manning screwed up his lips. "You know, there's something... last time I was here..."

"What?" Thor asked.

"It wasn't on your premises, but I saw somebody out there..."

Thor and Odin exchanged glances.

"Who?" Odin asked.

Manning squinted. "I don't know who. It was really nothing. Last week Thursday, when I was out to upgrade the controls on your gate and switch out the boards. Zeus was in the pool, you three were elsewhere. As I was leaving, turning right just out of the gate, I saw somebody walking out of the woods—not up here, but down past the end of the driveway. From the back. Brown hair, Dodgers cap. Maybe medium height."

"Somebody was walking out of the woods down there?" Odin said. "You didn't see fit to say anything?"

"It was just off the road. I assumed he was taking a piss."

"And you're just telling us now?"

"Hey—" Manning held up his hands. "Guys take pisses, yeah? I would've told you if the guy was dressed as Abe Lincoln or if I thought it was any kind of 5-0 or agency. That's who you've always been looking at as far as trouble. That's who the gates and cameras are for, according to you yourself. I'm not alerting you to every random guy taking a piss down the road."

"It's not his job," Thor snapped at Odin. "We hire him for surveillance and gates."

"But you're thinking about it enough to mention it now," Odin said.

"It's one of those things that gets weirder in hindsight," Manning said. "You know, your subconscious sees it and files it away. Then today when you call about some joker leaving a package, my subconscious says to me, *'Hey, Robert Manning, you remember the guy in a ball cap? Remember that guy?'* And now I'm telling you. But again—" He put his hand on his chest. He really didn't want to be in trouble with my guys.

"I know," Thor said. "We don't mean to get on you."

I sat there, watching him, not sure what to make of his story. Because, '*Hey, Robert Manning?*' Whose subconscious addresses them by their full name?

"A Dodger's cap and brown hair," Odin spat out. "That's a lot of *fucking-g* guys in this town."

"But it rules out a lot of guys," Manning said. "You take all the guys who might know where you four are hiding out with Isis and narrow it down to brown hair and Dodgers fandom..."

"And then narrow it down to those who are stupid enough to threaten Isis," Odin said.

"Wait—" Thor swore softly under his breath. "Sounds like fucking Bolo."

"Who's Bolo?" I asked.

Odin held up a hand. "What else?" he asked Manning. "Anything else? Shirt? Pants?"

Manning shook his head.

"Could it have been Bolo?" Odin barked. "You know him."

Manning shrugged.

"Who's Bolo?" I asked.

"No way. How the fuck would Bolo know we're here?" Thor asked.

Manning showed Thor empty hands. The universal gesture for, *What do I know?*

Odin put a hand on my shoulder. "He's...we'll tell you." He eyed Manning. "You can't say it was or wasn't Bolo."

"I don't know. It doesn't feel like Bolo's style. To skulk. But physically," Manning said. "He made only a slight impression. It could be nothing. But you've got eyes everywhere now. Look at this." He started sliding through screens on the notepad. We watched the camera views click around. "Terrible thing, that package. Blood." He quickly looked at Odin. "We all set?"

Odin slapped him on the back and they walked off together.

"If it's Bolo, we can handle it," Thor said.

"How well do you know A/V Robert Manning?" I asked.

"We know him pretty well," Thor said. "He's pulled us out of some hot situations. Looked out for us in the past." He turned to me. "You're not thinking…"

"No," I said. "But I don't like his whole calling me *miss* stuff. What's up with that?"

Thor frowned. "It wouldn't be him. Christ, if it's him…"

"I'm sure it's nothing," I said. "It seems a way to keep me at arm's length. I would never call my friend's significant other *mister*. '*Sorry to hear that, mister.*'"

"He's always been an ally," Thor said. "We considered pulling him in on a job once."

I nodded. That was the highest level of trust, pulling a guy in on a job.

Odin was back.

"Are you one hundred percent on Manning?" Thor asked him.

"*Manning?*" Odin asked.

"She got a weird hit off him," Thor said.

"Not weird, just…I'm jumpy," I said. "I'm going to freak out about everybody who isn't you."

Odin grabbed a suitcase out of the closet. Or, I thought it was a suitcase until he opened it up to reveal weapons, silencers, rope, a drill, and some other hardware. "You two stay here. I'm going to shake the trees for Bolo. See if I can figure out where he lives and pay him a little visit. I'll get Zeus at five and we'll regroup."

"What if it's not Bolo?" I asked.

"Then he has nothing to worry about. We need to handle this. Thor, get on Bolo's social media. Isis, keep working on the feather."

"I'm pretty sure it's pigeon," I said, trying not to think about how a drill might figure into paying Bolo a visit.

"Are you one hundred percent sure?" Odin asked.

"No, but seriously? The feather? I don't need busywork."

"Are you a trained *fucking-g* agent? Do you have some *fucking-*

g knowledge we don't have? Some knowledge that the feather is unimportant?"

"More of a hunch," I said.

"You will work on the feather," Odin snapped. "I want to know the species without a doubt. Take it to the university if you must." Odin left with the case, and Thor and I got iced teas and sat out on the porch, ready to continue our tasks.

"What's the deal with Bolo?" I asked him. "Who is he?"

Thor put his feet up on the railing. "He's a guy around the scene. He somehow knew—I don't know who from or how—that you like to be watched. You know..." *Watched while fucking,* he meant.

"Wait, he *knew* this? How would he know such a thing?"

"Not from any of us. Zeus thinks..." He paused here. "Well, we *have* had some semi-public sex, if you recall. That involved one of us watching. It's one of the risks that..."

"That makes it fun," I said, finishing his sentence for him. But he was right. There had been a few episodes of that. Car sex. Public park in the middle of the night sex. Sex in the storage basement at Guvvey's, the gangster restaurant. Yes, they knew I liked the danger of getting caught, and they knew I liked one of my guys watching. But not some random guy.

"There's also the fact that the four of us are a romantic unit. Some guys don't respect that. A guy like Bolo, he'd never go up to a man in a traditional couple and ask, '*Hey, can I watch you fuck your woman?*' But it's known that we're a foursome. So people make assumptions. It could be simple as that."

I nodded. "Even the Gigis had some shit to say about me liking manwiches."

Thor snorted. "You love manwiches."

"Only with you guys."

"Never with anyone else, baby. Ever." Thor looked hard into my eyes and reached for my hand. "This thing is as real as it gets."

This happy feeling of warmth came over me, and I smiled.

Being with my guys felt like being *held* in the most wonderful way, like being surrounded by an invisible cocoon of love and support from the fiercest and most amazing men on the planet. Even if I was out somewhere alone, I felt held like that. I sometimes couldn't believe how lucky I was.

Thor squeezed my hand. "Anyway, Zeus told Bolo to fuck off, and Bolo got a little creepy about it."

"Creepy how?"

Thor just shook his head.

"I want to know," I said. "Don't infantilize me. We're partners."

Thor let go of my hand and watched a squirrel run up one of the tall trees in front of the porch. "Demeaning. Dehumanizing toward you. As if it shouldn't matter what you want, or what we want. Like it's just a porn thing, what we've got going. It was almost as if Bolo thought he had a right to you. As though we had a duty to share you. That was Zeus's impression. He would've put Bolo in the hospital if Odin hadn't been there to break it up."

"He *attacked* him?"

"Let's just say Zeus corrected him in his thinking. We thought that was that."

"You should have told me," I said. "Does this sort of thing happen a lot?"

"Only the one time," Thor said.

"So you think it's him?"

"It seems likely."

"Is he...what's his background?" I asked. Meaning criminal background.

"Zeus went into his records. He's been in for auto theft. He's a car guy. Odin says car guys are more likely to be predatory, though. It's not on his record, but it doesn't mean it's not in his background. Criminal records tend to reflect less than eight percent of a person's actual crimes."

"How do you get a survey like that? Did somebody at Guvvey's do it?"

"Something like that."

"Maybe we have to stop doing public stuff," I said.

The squirrel perched on a tree branch in a kind of waiting mode. The Pacific Ocean sparkled in tiny bright blue patches through the branches.

"Not like we ever start out meaning to do public stuff," he said.

"We could stop groping each other in public places," I suggested.

Thor looked at me like I was bonkers.

I smiled.

"Whoever left the package," he said, "they'll be made an example of."

"What does *made an example of* mean?" I asked.

"Whatever Zeus and Odin decide it means," Thor said. "They'll find this guy."

"Maybe it's a sign," I said. "Your hideout's been here for a while. People are getting to know us."

"Are you on the Jerba thing again?" he asked.

"There's a bad apple in the barrel," I said.

"And we'll find it and take it out." Thor patted his lap. "Put your feet up here."

"I don't feel like fucking," I said.

Thor gave me a mock angry look.

"I don't."

"Do you not feel like getting your feet rubbed?"

"Yes," I said. "Wait, no." I put up my feet. "Whatever answer gets a foot rub." He started squishing the balls of my feet. I groaned. "Uhhhhh." The man knew his bones.

Ten minutes and two jelly feet later, I was scanning through diagrams of feathers.

"Crap," he said, tapping his iPad.

"What?" I asked.

"One of the midwives I back up in Santa Rosa. A risky breech baby delivery." He started typing. "It would be fine for her to have the baby at home if it wasn't a breech and if she didn't have so many health complications."

"Can't she go to the clinic?"

"She won't. Trouble with the law," he mumbled, typing an email, presumably. "The midwives have been trying to turn the baby, but it's a no go. I want to help her." He tapped one last time and sat back. "I feel like she's family—an outlaw sister. But I was hoping this would be better news."

"How long until labor?"

"We've got three weeks, maybe four. I'm going down there after the Prime. I've stashed oxygen and a new monitor with them."

Thor was so much calmer and way less reckless now that he was making a difference for people. His volunteer work in the clinic meant the world to him.

"Progress on the feather?"

"I'm stumped. It doesn't match anything online. I mean, it sort of does, but the afterfeather part isn't quite a pigeon."

"Looks like we're taking a trip to the university."

"Oh, come on. I know you're keeping me busy so that I don't worry."

He stood. "Everything's important."

An hour later, we were standing in the cool basement of a large university building asking directions to the ornithology lab from a young woman with a short afro and a tie-dyed shirt.

"There isn't an ornithology lab," she informed us.

"How about an ornithology grad student?" I asked.

"We're paying cash for an ID on a feather," Thor said.

The woman tilted her head quizzically. "How much?"

"How about three hundred?" Thor asked.

She paused in a way that suggested that was either a very good price or a very bad price. "Yeah, you can get an ID for that," she said finally.

Good price, then.

She led us to a hallway lined with doors, eventually stopping at one that was covered with cartoons that looked like they were cut out of a newspaper. Most of them were about mountain lions.

"He's a panther guy," she explained, "but he knows birds. You have to know birds as a panther guy because panthers eat birds."

Thor seemed amused by that.

The door was opened by a wiry, outdoorsy looking kid who appeared to be no older than sixteen. "What's the blood on this?" he asked, examining the feather through the baggie.

"We're running it. Pig's blood, we think," Thor explained. "It was left as a prank, so to speak."

The guy put the feather under a microscope. "Huh. Not... entirely common."

"I need everything interesting you can tell me about it." Thor pulled out a wad of twenties and shelled out $300 to the panther guy and another bunch of money to the woman who found him for us.

"This is really generous," she said. "Thank you."

"You need your answer in a hurry or something?" the panther guy asked. "I'll have to run a very specific round of tests on this one. How does seventy-two hours sound?"

"Can you give it to us in the next forty-eight hours?" He slapped a few more bills onto the table.

The panther guy smiled. Nothing like doing business with bank robbers.

Chapter Six

THERE WAS NO SIGN OF ZEUS OR ODIN WHEN WE GOT home. But on the upside, no creepy package on the front step.

"Pull out your piece," Thor said as we stepped out of the car. The guys liked to call their guns 'pieces.'

I pulled my silver pistol from my purse. Thor had his Sig pointed down by his leg.

"From now on, we clear the place all around. We clear every room before anything else. No surprises. You know how to do this."

"Yup." We'd been training.

We headed around through the shrubbery and scrub trees that grew on the rocky terrain around the house, a one-story rambler that was two-stories in the back due to the hill.

We crept past the lower patio, the sunken hot tub, the rustic outdoor shower.

The fierce wind streamed through Thor's bright blond hair and his gun flashed in the sunshine. He looked like a Viking Rambo.

I followed him, feeling like a mountain goat on high heels,

silver revolver at the ready. I'm sure we made quite the picture. Luckily, the foliage was thick enough that our neighbors couldn't see us unless they were really scrutinizing.

We slid in the back patio door and went from room to room, always with our backs to a wall and guns out, ensuring each was empty.

By the time we'd cleared the farthest bedroom, we heard a crash up front.

I stiffened.

Another crash. Like something breaking.

Thor and I exchanged glances.

"Should we sneak out the back way?" I asked.

He frowned. "Nope—we investigate. Steady and smart. You take low, I'll take high."

This meant that we'd appear in a doorway when he gave the signal, me crouched, him standing.

We crept into the side hall. My pulse raced as another crash sounded. Somebody was trashing the place! I caught Thor's blue gaze. His jaw was set, and he held the gun pointed upward in front of his face. He wasn't an agent by training like Odin and Zeus, but a life of vicious takeover robberies tends to give a guy skills, let's just say.

We reached the entrance and he nodded. We spun in. I crouched and pointed just in time to see Odin, arms crossed, watching Zeus hurl a vase at the fireplace. It exploded into a shower of shards.

"Christ!" Thor stood.

"We're home, honey," Odin said.

Zeus spun around, green eyes shining as though he were possessed. He still had his blue HVAC contractor jumpsuit on, but even a bulky one-piece couldn't hide the angry flex of his muscles. "Somebody has the gall to fucking threaten her? Some mother-fucker *threatens* her?"

"Oh, they'll wish they hadn't soon enough," Thor said. "Any location on Bolo?" he asked, wincing as Zeus drove a fist through the wall.

Odin looked on grimly. "No location on Bolo. Yet."

Thor grunted and holstered his Sig and I slipped my gun back in my purse, feeling a little freaked out about Zeus, who pulled his fist from the wall and punched again. Why weren't they stopping him?

Suddenly he swung his gaze to me. "Baby!" Zeus stomped over to me and wrapped me in his strong arms. He smelled like sawdust, motor oil, and man, I hugged him back, pressed against his massive chest, feeling the rapid rise and fall of his breath. "I didn't mean to scare you," he rasped, kissing my hair. "I didn't mean it." He pressed gentle hands onto my cheeks and looked into my eyes. "You okay?"

"Of course."

"God damn." He kissed me, and suddenly it was like a kiss with his whole body, meaty hands roaming and holding me everywhere, as though he had to touch every inch of me to ensure I was okay. He moved to planting feverish kisses on my cheek and neck.

"I'm okay," I whispered, enjoying his warm hands and lips on my skin. "We're okay."

"This guy goes down," he growled, pushing me up against a wall, kissing me, mauling me. It was unspeakably hot to be taken over by him in this state.

"I know," I said.

He forced my lips open in a bruising kiss, invading my mouth with his tongue, his heat, his lips, grinding the back of my head against the wall.

"I know you will," I said again, holding onto his rock-solid waist. Part of me was scared by his brutish protectiveness.

And part of me wanted him to take me wild.

With a groan, he lowered himself slightly and pressed the

outline of his rock-solid shaft between my legs, thick and hard as a fist. My belly tightened as he bore upwards, pressing himself into my sex, humping relentlessly.

"I have to…" He panted between kisses, seeming to forget what he was going to say.

"Yes," I whispered, clinging onto him, riding him as the electricity between my legs mounted. "Everything, baby—bring everything."

"I need to…" he moaned, practically fucking me right through my skirt. "If you like these clothes…"

"Do it," I whispered.

He stilled just long enough to grab the sides of my blouse and rip it asunder, pulling the stray pieces off me like tissue paper. Feverishly, he yanked my bra down, letting my breasts pop up, one of which he took into his sucking, panting mouth as he demolished the waistband of my skirt, stripping me the rest of the way with harsh efficiency.

The snaps on his jumpsuit clacked as he tore it clear off and rid himself of his underwear. "Yes," I whispered as he came back onto me, flattening me with his heat and bulk. He kissed and nuzzled my neck, abrading my skin, setting my libido on fire.

Somewhere nearby I heard the clink of glass and then the sound of a bottle cap coming off a bottle. Odin, or maybe Thor, signaling we had an observer.

Fuck, yeah. I nearly came right there.

A thick, meaty finger slid into my crotch. "Be ready, baby," he gusted. "Be ready." It was more a prayer than a command, because he so didn't want to wait.

Maybe he couldn't.

"Fuck me so hard," I said as he plundered me with his finger. I grabbed the back of his neck. "Take me right here. I'm so wet for you." I'm sure this fact was obvious to him, but he liked when I said it.

Firm hands gripped the bottoms of my thighs and he lifted me with a gust of breath and pressed me against the wall, kissing me.

I wrapped my legs around him and reached down to take his huge cock, gripping his steely shaft and pressing the bulbous tip of his cock into me. He sighed and drove into me the rest of the way, filling me mercilessly.

"Yes. Fuck me."

At first he fucked me slow and strong, all full of pent-up emotion. It was all the sweeter knowing somebody was watching me be completely taken and pleasurized, like the watcher was fucking me a little, too. Thor, I guessed. I could sometimes tell who was watching by the way their eyes felt all over my naked skin.

Zeus drove into me, holding me, owning me. I grabbed on.

He breathed in his rhythmic pant—*uh-uh-uh*.

"Everything," I whispered incoherently, meaning what I wanted and what he was and maybe a million other things.

He began to go harder, pistoning me into the wall, filling me with a dark, sparkly pain that spiraled the pleasure up to scary heights until I almost couldn't stand how beautiful it felt.

"God, Zeus!" I cried out as something fell off a nearby shelf and shattered on the floor. On he went. More glass stuff fell off and then my mind exploded apart in a wild orgasm that spun on and on.

"Goddess," he cried out, thrusting into me anew, crying out, and finally stilling.

Odin's phone rang.

We all stood by while he had a conversation that consisted of grunts and a thank you. He clicked off. "Bolo's at IHOP on Clister Avenue."

"Load up, we're going to the IHOP," Zeus said, stomping out of the room.

Odin opened the gun cabinet and strapped on an ankle holster. Thor got out a double shoulder holster.

"I'm going, too?" I asked.

"That's right," Odin said. "Hell if we're leaving you alone. What if he's not there? We stay together until this threat is handled."

Zeus returned in big black boots, cargo pants and a black T-shirt, short brown hair still mussed from sex. He looked hot and scary.

"Hey," said Odin, who was wearing the same thing. "You make us into *fucking-g* twins?" It was kind of a joke. My guys were always wearing T-shirts and cargo pants. They were very into cargo pants because of all the shit they could put in the pockets.

"Come on," Zeus said, not in any kind of mood for humor.

Twenty minutes later, Thor and I were waiting in the back seat of the SUV, which was parked in front of the International House of Pancakes just off Santa Monica Boulevard. Its steep chalet-style roof and giant wall of windows afforded a great view of Zeus and Odin storming into the place.

"There he is. Guy in the Dodgers cap at the middle table," Thor said.

I spotted him. The place was busy. Dinner rush. It was kind of like a silent movie, watching Zeus and Odin walk up. Watching the terrified cringe form on the face of Bolo, unmistakable even from outside.

"He knows he's fucked," Thor said. "He thinks Zeus would have no problem shooting him in the face right there in the restaurant. Zeus wouldn't do that, of course, especially not in front of kids, but that's the rep that Zeus has. He's not above exploiting it."

"I don't want some guy hurt if it's not him. I mean, creepy proposition, fine."

"Don't worry," Thor said. "They'll figure it out. This is their thing."

Bolo rose. The three of them were talking. Bolo gesturing.

"'*I'm innocent,*'" Thor said. "That's what Bolo's saying. Look at his hands. His shoulders. '*I know nothing.*'"

"Then you *fucking-g* prove it," I said, taking Odin's part.

Thor smiled.

"Isis is so beautiful," Thor said, playing Bolo's part now. "I lost my mind when I said that thing about watching, but I didn't send the box."

I snorted. "You prove it or the clouds will *fucking-g* weep as we gouge out your eyes with a small, shit-covered stick."

"Odin would never say that," Thor said. "A shit-covered stick."

"I know."

"Bolo will try to prove his innocence, though," Thor said.

"Guilty until proven innocent," I said.

"Man insulted you mightily," Thor reminded me.

We watched Zeus walk Bolo away from the table. Odin flicked a bill onto it and followed.

"Here is your *fucking-g* money," I whispered.

They headed out the doors and across the parking lot. Bolo was a big guy, but he was dwarfed by Odin and Zeus, who both stood well over six feet. They seemed to be heading toward our SUV. I wasn't sure how I liked the idea of actually having to talk with Bolo, considering his indecent proposition.

Zeus came around, yanked open the driver's side door, and got in.

Odin opened the passenger side door and shoved Bolo in. His hat fell off onto his lap.

"Eyes on the front," Odin said, getting in and squishing him to the side. "You don't get to look at her."

"I didn't leave anything on your porch," Bolo said. "I was in Vegas until the morning. I just got back today. Thor—"

"You're not dealing with Thor, you're dealing with me and Odin." Zeus started up the truck. "If you're telling the truth, I'll find out." He peeled out of the parking lot.

I felt a little sorry for Bolo. You could practically smell the fear on him. Was this the kind of man to leave a threatening package? Or to dress as Abe Lincoln and leave a warning?

Twenty minutes later, we were all traipsing up to Bolo's long-term room at the Hampshire Hotel. Bolo swiped his key card and swung the door open.

The place was trashed.

Odin sat Bolo on the couch. "Babysit him. And Isis sits here." He pointed at a chair across from Bolo, which was pretty much the last place I wanted to sit. "And if you so much as look at her, Thor will break your fingers."

"How about if I sit here?" I nodded toward chair off to the side.

Odin growled his grudging assent, not in the mood to argue. "Be grateful for her benevolence."

Thor pulled out his Sig and set a foot on the arm of the couch, gun in hand, looking every inch the mercenary, while Odin and Zeus poked around. They were looking for the paper and markers.

"Ask Double D," Bolo said. "He was with me."

"Yeah, yeah, yeah," Odin said. "Double D never lies."

Zeus grabbed a pizza box and opened it up. Just crusts. He smelled one.

"That was from before I left," Bolo said. "I swear! You can call PizzaMiza."

"I don't need to," Zeus said, smashing it between his fingers, creating a small stream of crumbs that fell down to the floor. "Wednesday."

"Yes! Which is when we left. See?"

"Only proves you're a slob," Zeus said.

"How'd you know that was Wednesday's crust?" Bolo asked, careful to look anywhere except at me. "Why not Tuesday's or Thursday's?"

"Shut up," Thor said, ice blue eyes fixed on the guy's face.

Odin came in with a to-go coffee. "This is from today," he said.

"Yes, yes!" Bolo exclaimed. "I bought it before I left, with a credit card."

"You have a receipt?" Zeus asked.

"No, but online. I can prove it online."

Odin pulled out his phone. "Go into your credit card and show us the charge."

Bolo tapped the screen with shaking hands. Eventually, he got his password right and got into his account. "There! Six in the morning. Starbucks. Grand Mahaj hotel."

"Where's the hotel charge?" Odin asked.

"I paid cash for the room."

Thor snorted. "You paid cash for the hotel room and not the coffee? Why would you do that?"

"I lost all my money the previous night," Bolo said.

Odin frowned. "Abe Lincoln mean anything to you?"

"Umm...he was a president?"

"That's it?" Odin said.

Bolo looked confused. "He's on the penny?"

Eventually we left.

When we were back in the Nav, I asked, "How can you tell today's coffee from yesterday's?"

Zeus seemed calm for maybe the first time that day. "State of the dairy. Evaporation rate. In a heavily air-conditioned environment like that room, you'd have a ring above the liquid line. It was maybe five hours old. No more. And he has a coffee maker there. It did make me think he didn't wake up there this morning."

"And the pizza crust?"

He shrugged.

I said, "You have a mobile lab I didn't see?"

"I have the power of observation," he said. "And that Lincoln stuff. He didn't know. They could be unrelated, but I don't think either offense was him."

"Now what?" Thor asked.

"Home. I'm going to check out his alibi, but I suspect it'll check out," Zeus said. "Once he's cleared, we're beating the bushes at Guvvey's. This is somebody from our circle."

"Agreed," Odin said.

Thor nodded, snapping his holster.

My guys seemed energized, alive, sparkling, almost, in a way I had never seen and didn't quite understand.

Chapter Seven

MOST NIGHTCLUBS IN LOS ANGELES HAVE THINGS LIKE, oh, valet parking and front doors. But not Guvvey's, the nightclub of the crème de la crème of the criminal elite. Instead of a front door, there is a scary parking ramp to park in and a scuffed-up secret door that takes you underground into foreboding series of tunnels, eventually leading you to an elevator that whisks you upwards.

Even the floor Guvvey's occupies isn't a real floor. Zeus explained once that it's a between-floors floor. The regular elevators don't stop at it.

Zeus swung a protective arm around me, and Thor set a hand on the small of my back as we walked into Guvvey's. Odin trailed behind, on the lookout no doubt. I was used to being flanked by my guys, but nothing like this. It gave me the shivers.

It was midnight—early still—but the place was full of people and thrumming with music. We moved across the dark expanse and took a booth, the four of us, with me sandwiched in between Zeus and Odin.

My guys were on high alert, looking discreetly all around. I ordered a champagne and they ordered sodas.

"Wait," I said, "change mine to soda if we're not drinking."

"No, keep her champagne," Zeus said, sending the waiter away. "You deserve it," he said. "You get to drink what you prefer. We're on the job." He touched a finger under my chin and lowered his voice. "We won't let anything happen to you, Isis." He paused, seeming like he was about to say something, and I had the wild thought that he was going to say *we love you*, but he simply let his hand slide to my bare shoulder where it rested, heavy and warm. He smiled and kissed me. "You look beautiful."

"Thank you." I was wearing a red, one-shoulder dress they all really liked. My guys were in sports coats, all the better to conceal lots of weaponry. Not that you needed to conceal at Guvvey's, but they were packing an unusual amount.

"You think he's going to show up?"

"Very likely," Odin said. "He needs a reaction. That's the only function that package served—to get a reaction. Once it circulates we're here, he's going to come."

"Ugh," I said.

"It's shocking," Thor said. "That anybody could possibly think they would get away with this. They know we have resources."

"Not the extent of them, perhaps." Odin said, and then he eyed Zeus. "It's been so long. Playing the hunter."

"It feels good," Zeus said, waving at a man across the room, standing at the bar. "I'm going to talk to Clarence on the Dodgers aspect." He got up and walked off.

Odin nudged Thor. "Look—Henry."

"Who's Henry?" I asked.

"Go-to gossip man," Thor said, nodding at a blond man in a blue suit. "Anything going around the grapevine hits Henry. If anybody is unduly fascinated with you."

"You talk to him, Thor," Odin said. "He's more comfortable with you."

"He's more frightened of you," Thor said.

"Comfort is best for now. Go at him soft, and then I'll go at him if you think he's holding back."

"Right." Thor gave me a kiss on the cheek and went over to talk to Henry.

The drinks arrived. I was glad for the champagne now.

"We'll find him," Odin said. "It's what we do. I think a lot of people don't understand that. We could find people on the other side of the world."

Find them and kill them. But Odin didn't say that, but it's how they'd hooked up with Thor—Odin had been sent by their clandestine government agency ZOX to kill Thor, back when Thor was a relief organization doctor who'd had the misfortune of witnessing something he shouldn't have. When Odin learned who Thor was and what he'd seen—they would never tell me what, exactly—he'd decided to protect Thor from ZOX instead of executing him. Then Zeus had been sent to kill them both.

Odin had fought Zeus and brought him around to the idea that ZOX was fucking up and that Thor shouldn't be killed. Eventually, another agent had been sent to kill all three of them. They killed that person. It was at that point they knew they'd have targets on their backs forever. Which was when their path of vengeance robbery began.

Matteo came over and slid in next to Odin, looking angry. "This stalker is still out there? Everybody's talking about it."

"What'd you hear?" Odin asked. "From who?"

"Vanessa Foy heard about it and she's telling people."

"From Bolo. Fuck," Odin said. "That was fast."

"We have big plans next week," Matteo said. "Do we need to put them off?"

"Hell no." Zeus slid in on the other side of me, squeezing in close. He brushed a strand of hair from my forehead and kissed me. "Heya, baby," he said.

"Hey," I whispered.

"Like that. We can't have your attentions divided," Matteo

said. "There's a lot of recon to do in the next few days, and here you are conducting some side investigation? Not that I blame you."

"We got this handled," Zeus said. "You watch how sizzling fast we catch this guy."

"I sat on the bank on my own all afternoon," Matteo said. "I didn't mind taking your shifts, but it can't happen anymore."

"The Prime is important to our family," Zeus said. "We've got the bandwidth to do both. Nobody fucks with us."

"Yeah, yeah, yeah," Matteo said, looking off at Thor across the room.

"Yeah, yeah, *yeah*?" Zeus said. "You got a problem?"

I stiffened in my seat, thinking Zeus might haul off and hit Matteo. The veins on Zeus's neck became dangerously defined. I was starting to feel dizzy off the sheer testosterone.

"Nobody fucks with you. We all get that," Matteo said. "But reacting *is* letting them fuck with you. They are fucking with you already."

"You're saying we should let this go unchallenged?" Zeus said.

"No, I'm saying somebody is fucking with you, and I'm pointing out that you're dancing like a puppet. That is the feeling I'm getting off you right now."

"A puppet?" Zeus said, voice all scary calm.

Gulp.

"Yeah, like a puppet," Matteo said. "As in, you're not in control of your actions, and that has the potential to jam up our job with the Prime. So maybe we should postpone it so you can put your attention on this thing."

"The HVAC project will be over with if we wait," Odin said. "Zeus won't be on the inside anymore. We lose our advantage if we postpone."

"We make a new plan," Matteo said. "We still have the codes. And not to be insensitive, but..." He looked over at me. "You're the driver. We can't be inside there relying on you if there's a potential of somebody chasing you off or..."

"Gruesomely attacking and killing me?" I asked. "Because that would really mess the job up."

"Not to be *fucking-g* insensitive," Odin bit out, offended.

Matteo shrugged. I liked that he was being forthright. And yes, I'd be alone out there. The guys would be in the ducts.

I looked over at Zeus. "It's not a bad point."

Zeus grunted. "That's why we'll nab this guy before the job."

Matteo gazed across the bar. "I don't want to postpone, either. But I want to go in right."

I followed his gaze over to a stately woman in a silver gown who was glaring at Matteo. Macy, one of the Gigis, aka the Giraffes. She was flanked by Jenny Gigi and Angel Gigi. The girl jewel-thief gang.

Macy pushed off the bar and headed our way, followed by her friends in a formation like three fighter jets. Angel wore a yellow party dress with a tiara—she always seemed to go for tiaras. Jenny had on a slinky dress that was practically poured onto her.

"Oh, God," Matteo mumbled under his breath.

I sat up with the sudden sensation that I was in high school, and the cool girls were coming. Even the way they walked was cool.

The Gigis had asked me to join up with them some time ago, when they had been down a driver. It had enraged my guys to no end, but I'd been flattered as hell. I didn't want to join their gang, but I sort of wanted to be friends with them.

"I hear you found trouble, Isis," Macy said to me. "Some asshole leaving a bloody feather for you."

"Bloody feather and a creepy note," I said.

She shook her head. "That's messed up."

She looked at Zeus. Then Odin. Then me. Macy was looking at everybody except for Matteo. "You all rustle up any leads?"

"We're pursuing several good avenues," Zeus said.

She snorted. "You sound like a cop." Finally, she eyed Matteo.

"You all look pretty cozy."

Matteo shrugged.

"Up to something?"

"You know we can't divulge that, baby," Matteo said.

"Don't call me baby," Macy snapped. "You lost that privilege."

"I'll stop saying it out loud then," Matteo said, "but I won't stop saying it in my mind. Because you're always going to be my baby. And every time I see you, I'll be thinking, *'Here's the woman I love.'* And I fucked up, and I get that I'm in the doghouse now, but you won't stop me from feeling how I do."

"Could you not make a scene?" Macy said. "I'm just here to offer Ice some assistance."

"I'm not making a scene," Matteo said. "But fine, if it makes you feel better for me to posture and pretend, I can do that. Because I hear what you're asking of me, and I'm going to honor that. I'll sit here like a hard guy. You want that? For me to be a liar with my eyes? I'll be a liar with my eyes, fine." He crossed his arms and got a hard look in his eyes.

Angel said, "Too little, too late."

"I was never a liar," Matteo said.

"Just stop." Macy threw up a hand and addressed me again. "If you need an assist in catching this creep, we're all over it. Look, Jenny had a stalker, and we put that guy down. This is a man's game out here, or at least, a lot of guys think it is. I know you God Pack guys are cool, but—"

"We got it handled," Zeus said. "But if you hear anything, or if anybody has been buzzing about Isis, we're interested."

"Lots of people are buzzing about Isis. What do you expect?" Macy said. "But we'll keep our ears and eyes open."

"Thanks," I said. "I really appreciate that."

"Sure," Macy said. "It's not Jenny's guy, I'll tell you that."

Angel snorted.

Matteo grinned. "It was a motherfucking thing of beauty to behold when they caught Jenny's stalker."

Macy glared at him. "What happened to hard guy?"

"You know what happened to hard guy," Matteo said.

Angel looked around the table. "You guys are coming up on a job," she said. "I can feel it."

Thor strolled up behind them. "Sorry, ladies, you'll have to read about it in the paper with everyone else."

Macy rolled her eyes as Thor shoved in and sat on the other side of Zeus. Then she turned, and the three of them walked off, fighter jet style.

I narrowed my eyes at Matteo. "What *happened* with you and Macy?"

Matteo shrugged.

"He slept with another woman," Odin said.

"Yikes," I said.

"Don't say it like that," Matteo said. "It wasn't my fault."

"Not your fault?"

"No. We were gearing up to hit this mansion in Malibu, and I got an in as a cable guy, and the lady of the house, she wanted a go with me. I wasn't going to fuck her. I was just acting into her, but when you're acting into somebody? When you're a guy? Sometimes biology just takes over."

"That's your excuse?" Odin asked, incredulous. "Biology took over? Is that what you told Macy?"

"Yeah, that's what I told Macy," Matteo said.

"That's your problem," Odin said. "You're not taking responsibility."

"I'm not saying I didn't do it. It was me," Matteo said. "I did it, but it was biology. I wasn't into her."

Thor grinned. "Yet you were."

"Biology didn't fuck the woman," I said.

"This job'll let me show her how I feel. That's what giving her the Liz Taylor diamonds is. She's wanted those jewels since she was a little girl."

"That's nice," I said. "But she also needs to know that you're taking responsibility, like Odin said."

"I don't see how I can take more responsibility than putting myself in danger to get her the prize of the century."

"If I were her, I'd be more interested in an assurance that the fucking won't happen again," I said. "How does she know biology won't take you over again?"

Matteo frowned.

"It's like the parole board," Odin said. "They don't give a shit about excuses. They need to see you have insight into how you fucked up and that you have control over your own actions going forward."

"But sometimes it really does happen like that," Matteo said. "You can't help it."

"Then why should she get back with you?" I asked.

"I won't put myself in that situation again, that's why," Matteo said.

Odin rolled his eyes. "It's not the situation that fucked the other woman."

I added, "What if you get into that situation accidentally? Why should Macy trust you?"

Odin pointed at him. "You need to *fucking-g* ponder that decision-making process with the woman you cheated with. You need to look at yourself and why you want to pretend your biology controls your dick, because you know what? It doesn't. You have a worldview that says you're sometimes not responsible for your own actions. But you are, Matteo. You need to look inside yourself and ask, '*What do I get out of that worldview? What does it mean if I'm responsible for my actions? What do I fear if I accept that as the truth?*'"

I watched Odin, stunned. Impressed.

"Jesus Christ!" Matteo said. "Seriously?"

"What do you lose if you accept that you alone control your own actions?" Odin pressed. "You ponder that."

"God," Matteo said. "It's not enough to be in mortal danger

robbing the Prime? Because I don't know how to do this other shit."

"Everybody knows how to do it," Odin said. "You don't want to."

My phone buzzed just then. Which was strange, because everybody who had that number was with me. I pulled it out and looked at the screen. Unavailable.

"Somebody's calling me," I said stupidly. You weren't supposed to have phones in Guvvey's, but the owner changed the rules once he got re-addicted to Tetris.

Zeus grabbed it. "Answer it normally. A simple hello." He put it on speaker and set it in front of me and then took out his own phone.

"Hello?" I said.

My guys all bent in.

A distorted male voice. "I'm coming for you, Isis."

My belly dropped through me.

Odin and Zeus flew up from the table, looking all around the bar.

Thor slid closer and swirled the air with his finger. *Talk more.*

"Who is this? What do you want?" I asked, trying to keep my voice from shaking.

"You know what I want," the voice said. "It's only a matter of time 'til I get it."

I looked up into Thor's blue eyes, uncharacteristically grim now. "Who is this?" I asked.

"Bring your lipstick," the voice said.

The line went dead. I didn't even want to touch the thing.

"Christ," Matteo said.

Thor took a deep breath and moved in closer to me. "You're okay."

Zeus and Odin were out of sight. "Where'd they go?" I asked.

"The thinking is always that this kind of stalker gets his jollies out of seeing you react, seeing us react," Thor said. "So they're looking for people acting suspiciously. People watching us, people hurrying away. Just taking in the crowd. Everybody here is now a suspect."

"I hope you all got a lot of photos of this crowd," Matteo said.

"Defo," Thor said.

Matteo snorted. "Such a mindfuck to see those two acting like cops."

"It's weird for me, too." Thor turned his gaze to his soda, half gone, in the highball glass. "Bring your lipstick," he repeated.

"What does it mean?" I asked, feeling all shaky. I drained my drink.

Matteo furrowed his brow. "Well, you *do* wear lipstick, I guess."

"Yeah." I actually wore lipstick a lot, and I reapplied it a lot. When I went from redhead to blonde, it gave me a whole new class of makeup to use, including frosty pink, something you couldn't pull off as a redhead.

The Gigi's and I had put lipstick on together in the bathroom...could it be them with a voice distorter? I hated the idea, but I looked around, wondering. At least we knew it wasn't Matteo.

I swallowed, thinking I really was visible and notable these days, what with the bright colors I favored and being a woman with three men. I felt almost ashamed for the first time. I'd clawed my way into this life I loved, but maybe I had taken too much.

Thor had a faraway look in his eyes.

"What?" But right then, I remembered. Venus, the woman who'd been with them before, had written her suicide note in lipstick.

"It's probably nothing," he said.

Zeus was back. "Fucker's watching. He's got to be." He picked up my phone and smashed it into a brick pillar to the side of the table. His intensity made me feel worried, but also like an army was on my side. A powerful army of stormy guys.

"We're okay," Thor said to me. He slung his arm around my

shoulders.

I sucked in a breath, heart pounding. Of all the threats we'd encountered, this one was the scariest, because it felt like it was coming from our people. I thought about the cozy sheep farm I'd left behind, the place I could never return to. Nothing ever happened there, but it was safe. And I thought about the sun-drenched hotel on the Tunisian island. I rested my head on his shoulder.

"Stop looking scared, baby," Zeus said. He slid in on the other side of me and put an arm around me. "You're giving whoever it is what he wants."

"But I am scared," I said.

"And *you're* looking pissed," Matteo pointed out to Zeus.

Zeus looked more than pissed. "Somebody dies," he growled. "And the lipstick? Not loving it."

"Everybody knows about that part," Matteo said. "It's common knowledge."

"It's a taunt," Zeus growled. "Somebody dies. I'm telling you."

"Can you get something from the phone carrier?" Matteo asked. "A trace or some such? On the number that called?"

"They called from a burner. No way would they be so stupid not to," Zeus said. "Fuck! How'd they get her number?"

"We're hitting the Prime Royale in six days," Matteo said.

Zeus turned to him. "We're not rethinking that."

"We don't *have* to hit the Prime," I said.

"Yes, we do," Zeus barked. "Nobody messes with our own. Canceling this job, it's like giving in to a terrorist. We don't give into ZOX, and we don't give into stalkers."

Odin strolled up with a fierce expression, sexy in his black suit. "That SIM card had better be intact."

"They called from a burner," Zeus said.

"I'd like to look all the same," Odin said. "And let's press our contacts a little harder."

Zeus grunted.

I'd seen this before—Odin sometimes stepped up when Zeus got emotional. Zeus lacked a certain amount of impulse control. Or maybe he let himself lack it, knowing Odin was there. So much of our group was symbiotic, I sometimes didn't know where one of us started and the other ended.

"They could've triangulated it from our numbers. It's not hard," Zeus said.

"Oh, is that how?" Odin said. "Too bad the phone's in pieces."

"You guys," I said. "We're going to be okay. I have total faith."

A waitperson appeared with a broom and dustpan.

Odin took the implements from him. "Bring me a baggy, okay?" He grabbed a cocktail napkin and started cleaning off the dustpan.

Zeus swore under his breath.

I fit my hands around him, holding him from the side. "I don't feel worried," I whispered. I didn't have a word for how I felt at the moment. Except maybe kaleidoscopic. I snuggled in more tightly.

He grabbed my hair and gave me a deep kiss, plying my lips open, pulling me hard against him. "Nobody fucks with you."

"Except you," I said.

"I want to fuck you right now," he said. "I feel wild, goddammit. But..." He grabbed my knees and pulled me onto his lap so that my legs were completely around him. "We've got a motherfucking stalker to catch. He pulled out his phone and punched in a number so hard I was shocked the screen didn't crack.

I kissed his neck. When I shifted, I could feel his cock, rock hard in his pants. He launched into an intense, mumbled conversation. Pressuring somebody about the fingerprints.

Odin finished gathering up the phone pieces into the baggie.

"Just a little more time," Thor said quietly to Matteo. "Let's see where we are tomorrow with all this."

So Thor was open to putting the Prime Royale on the back burner. That was a relief.

Chapter Eight

Whatever Zeus had done to speed up the fingerprint processing had worked, because an hour later, the four of us were speeding down a highway toward Tivendale Heights, a suburb an hour northeast of LA, after a quick stop to change out of our clubbing clothes and get more weaponry.

The lights blurred by and the rain streaked sideways across the windows in spite of the wipers working double time.

They'd gotten a hit on one of the sets of fingerprints—a guy named Ingvey. He had a sexual assault arrest record.

Perfect, Zeus had said.

That was one way to look at it, I guess.

Odin sat in the front next to Zeus, as usual. He was noodling around on his smartphone, digging into Ingvey's history.

"It's all *fucking-g* foot stuff with this Ingvey," Odin said.

I had my head on Thor's shoulder in the back, legs curled sideways. Thor's face was lit blue by the screen of his iPad. He was emailing back and forth with Mexico, which was never a good sign. I could feel his tension building. I sat up and tucked his hair behind his ear. Thor hadn't shaved for a while, and the blond scruff on his face made him more exotic in a kind of Scandinavian way, like you could imagine him traipsing through the moonlit snow in badass fur boots.

"Everything okay?" I asked.

"Lupe, my risky breech, is stressing," Thor said.

"You can't leave," Odin barked from the front.

"I won't. She has at least three weeks. Unless she goes early. But she won't," he added quickly.

Silence in the SUV. It would be bad to leave before the Prime, but in spite of what Odin had said, we all knew Thor needed to do this. Thor tended to unravel when he wasn't able to be his doctor self. Also, we all felt a special bond with Lupe due to her fugitive status. She was like our adopted sister.

"This makes zero *fucking-g* sense," Odin bit out. "Ingvey's a foot fetishist. What self-respecting foot fetishist would target Isis?"

"*Excuse* me?" I protested.

"Not that you don't have attractive feet, Isis, but you're not what I'd imagine as the object of a foot fetishist."

"What are you saying?"

Odin twisted around in the front seat to give me one of his smoldering looks. "That you dishonor our gang cloud tattoo with your chipped pink toenail polish." He turned back to the screen. "Stalking and threatening. It doesn't feel like the work of a foot fetishist. The feather, the note. The feet, the way such a man operates..." He trailed off, consumed with these psychological variables. "And when you look at what Ingvey has posted on boards," he added.

"You know a lot about foot fetishists?" I asked.

"I know a lot about every kind of person," Odin said simply.

"It's disturbing," Thor said, not looking up from his tablet. Thor was only half with us. That patient was worrying him.

"Isis has beautiful feet," Zeus said. "And I am going to tear off his balls for threatening her."

"You need to calm yourself down," Odin said.

I caught Zeus's eyes in the mirror, so full of anguish and rage and energy like a wild god. He looked intense and alone, strapped into the driver's seat, face pulsing light and dark from the headlights of passing cars, muscular hands dwarfing the steering wheel. I felt like if he wanted to, he could just rip apart the whole vehicle. I recalled the steely feel of his cock at the restaurant. I wondered if he was still hard.

"We don't know that it's him," Odin added. "We'll figure it out. They take people off investigations they're too close to for a reason, Zeus. We do it right."

"We *will* do it right." Zeus's chest rose and fell with force. "Whoever did this will not survive the heat of my goddamn fire." He was getting himself more and more agitated. "I will rain hell on anybody who even looks at her wrong."

"Odin has dibs on pulling out his guts like fishing rope, though," I said.

Odin grinned.

Zeus frowned.

"I have total faith in you," I said softly.

Zeus growled.

"When we enter his home, we'll figure it out. We'll inspect his shit, and we'll know," Odin said.

Which seemed like the last thing Zeus was capable of at the moment, on account of his fugue state of protectiveness. I could see that Odin, for one, didn't like it. I suddenly wished very much that we weren't speeding down a wet, rainy highway with me strapped into the backseat and Zeus strapped into the driver's seat. I wanted to feel him, to feel his fire, and to soothe him. I leaned forward and rubbed his shoulder.

Zeus shot a glance at me in the rearview mirror, gaze hooded, like he felt my desire. He gusted out a breath. "...just don't want you scared."

Odin looked at Zeus, then back at me. "Isis. Come up here," he said. "You need to sit in the middle of us."

"We're on the highway," I said.

Odin tilted his head and gave me an eagle-eye look.

"Never mind," Zeus said. "I'm driving."

Odin eyed me again. "Zeus needs to feel you and know that you are okay."

Zeus grunted in protest. "I'm driving."

"She's going to sit next to you, not suck your cock," Odin said.

I specifically didn't look over at Thor, who was a big fan of orgasms while driving. Or at least he had been, when he was on his recklessness jag before he got the clinic job.

"You'd want that, right?" Odin asked Zeus. "You want her up here?"

Zeus seethed out the windshield, like he could see Ingvey's face on the road in front of us. "Yeah," he grated.

Odin and I locked gazes. He didn't need to say anything more. Odin wanted me to help calm down Zeus. He thought that my touch would calm him. Like Zeus was this large and highly distressed beast, which I supposed he was.

I unbuckled my seatbelt and crawled up between them. Zeus hissed out a sigh of relief as I settled in next to him and pressed flush to him. He grabbed the back of my hair and pulled me closer. I wrapped my arms around his meaty chest as Odin buckled me in.

Zeus started talking about how they were going to keep me safe, and I trusted him on that. His fury hadn't kept him from brilliantly assessing every last clue inside Bolo's trashed rooms.

Odin leaned over to me and whispered in my ear, "Touch his skin. You need to touch his skin."

"What are you saying to her? Because I'm talking," Zeus barked.

"Sorry." Odin sat back and directed his attention out the passenger-side window.

I snaked my hand under Zeus's shirt and touched his firm, lightly furred belly, pressing my hand into his warm skin.

"Baby," Zeus breathed into my hair. His breathing seemed to calm and even out, just from my touch.

Odin put a hand on my leg, squeezed once. It was so weirdly observant of Odin to know that would happen.

I wedged my other hand a little ways in between the seat and Zeus's back. He kissed my head and moved his non-driving hand to my neck. "You feel so good," he breathed, sliding his hand down over my shoulder, cupping it. "You feel so good, and you smell so good," he said.

"Thank you." I snuggled into him, keeping my hand splayed over his firm belly, feeling the hard ridges of his muscles and the light, springy hairs.

We drove on into the night toward Ingvey in Tivendale Heights. Would he be our guy? Odin apparently had his doubts.

The dark back seat glowed with the soft light from Thor's iPad, the front with passing headlights, all to the soft chant of wipers sloshing back and forth and tires on wet road.

There in the dark I moved my palm in a circle over the contours of Zeus's belly. I could tell where the line of hairs that led to his cock started, but I didn't follow that treasure trail. This wasn't that kind of touching. I was just giving him reassurance. Skin-to-skin contact. They've done studies where skin-to-skin contact calms blood pressure, anger, all the freak-out markers; Thor would have the clinical term for it. Anyway, that's what I was concentrating on. I could tell I was helping him.

Like I was the Zeus whisperer.

Odin and Zeus didn't have to know how turned on I was—this was supposed to be a comforting thing, not a sexual thing. But every time my fingers strayed over that line of hair, all I wanted to do was press my hand down into Zeus's pants and take his giant, hard cock in my hand and my mouth and squeeze and lick and suck it.

I imagined him grabbing my hair and pushing my head down farther onto him the way I liked, forcing me to take him deeper. Thrusting and fucking my hand and mouth. I wanted to hear him go *uh-uh-uh* and lose all sense of everything. I wanted to feel all that fucking energy inside him build up and unspool.

The best would be if I could get my hands around his ass and squeeze his ass cheeks. That sometimes drove him wild.

Then I changed the thought—I'd squeeze his ass cheek with one hand, while I squeezed the root of his cock with the other. I loved how rigid it would get when I did that, like pure steel. Sucking Zeus's cock was like riding a tidal wave, but way hotter. And it ended better.

"Ice," Zeus grated, startling me.

"What?" I came to my senses and realized I was squeezing a handful of skin, practically taking a chunk out of his abs. "Oh, sorry."

"Fuck," he whispered, voice husky. "Fuck. It felt good." He looked down at me with a wild light in his eyes.

"Let's hit the next rest stop," Odin said.

The next thing I knew, the blinker was on.

Zeus moved his hand to my head again and squeezed my hair. "Ice," he panted.

"Yeah?" I said.

"Where're we going?" Thor asked.

"Rest stop," Zeus said, barreling down the exit ramp.

"The idea is to *fucking-g* slow *down* on the exit," Odin complained as Zeus sped toward the lonely building. Zeus slowed just before he squealed into a parking place.

The rest stop was dark and nearly deserted; only a couple of other cars were there. Not surprising considering it was 3:12 a.m.

Picnic tables were clustered off to the side under a towering light that illuminated the raindrops, though it was raining so hard, they weren't drops at all—more like fat, bright dashes of water, streaking through the slim cones of light and down into the darkness. Beyond the picnic area lay a dim expanse—grass with the occasional tree—and beyond that, more trees.

"We'll be right back." Zeus unbuckled his seatbelt and then

mine. He opened the door and got out. The rain pounded on his head and back.

"It's storming out there," I said as the rain splashed in on his empty seat.

He bent back into the car, panting, short brown hair dripping onto his forehead. "Come with me, Ice." He leaned in farther and kissed me roughly.

I laughed and grabbed his soaking wet shoulders. The rain was cold, but Zeus was warm, hot, and hard.

This stalker had brought out something new in Zeus—a weird, wild intensity.

I approved.

Chapter Nine

ZEUS WAS ALREADY PULLING ME OUT OF THE CAR.

"I need us to go out into the darkest part of that field out there," he gasped between kisses, like he'd die if it didn't happen.

"We'll wait," Odin said casually from the backseat

Zeus grabbed my ass and picked me clear up there in the pounding rain.

I locked my legs around his waist.

His steely cock ground into my sex.

"Yes," I whispered, gasping into another kiss.

I no longer cared about the rain.

He hiked me up and nuzzled my breast through my wet shirt, smushing around the fabric.

He was like a bear trying desperately to get into a tent and not understanding about the zipper.

I ripped apart my shirt, letting the buttons fly. I need the abrasive yumminess of Zeus's whiskery cheeks on my tender breasts.

I wanted the bear *in the tent*.

He brought his face to my dripping wet chest and rubbed his whiskers all over me, and then he took a nipple in his mouth and sucked like mad.

I balled my fists in his hair, squeezing, pulling, wrenching, as though his hair was a gas pedal and if I squeezed tightly enough while grinding hard enough against his cock, he'd go faster, harder, stronger.

"Jesus," he said, kissing up my neck. He stepped away from the SUV, and in one feverish and fluid motion, he hauled me up over his shoulder, firefighter style.

"Hey!" I gasped. The world was upside down.

He carried me like that out past the rest stop building and into the expanse beyond the picnic area where the lights didn't shine.

We headed deeper into the darkness, rain pounding, Zeus in total *Clan of the Cave Bear* mode. Everything seemed to be getting further away. The lights, the world. Rain beat down onto my back as he rounded a tree and flipped me back into his arms. He kneeled then, gently laying me out on the wet, muddy ground. "I hate that he fucking called you on your phone. I had to pulverize that thing. I don't care."

"Come here," I gasped, pulling him to me by his shirt. Instead, he broke away from my grip and stood over me, towering over me, chest heaving, cock straining through his soaking wet cargo pants.

A deep and primal part of me understood what was happening. It was as if, after the phone call, he had to claim me all over again. Something tightened deep in my belly at the thought. He ripped the shirt right off himself as if to confirm it and began to unbuckle his pants.

"If you're not naked in two seconds, those pants are getting destroyed, too."

I undid my jeans. Shirts and skirts are one thing, but it's hard to find jeans you really love.

Even though it was dark, I could see him perfectly, standing over me, naked, cock shining, watching me wriggle out of the jeans legs, trembling with excitement.

"Hurry it up," he growled. He'd tossed all of his clothes aside.

Later he'd be mad when he couldn't find them, but later didn't exist to him right now.

The mud felt cool and slippery under my ass as I pulled off my jeans. My foot splashed in a cool puddle. He snatched my clothes from my hands and tossed them aside, too; they were illuminated mid-air by a flash of lightning.

"Spread your legs for me," he whispered. "Touch yourself."

I parted my legs for him and pressed one hand to my slick pussy, sliding a finger around in my hot juices. I brought my other hand to my breast.

"Yeah, do that, too."

Zeus always liked when I touched myself really intensely and thoroughly.

"Fuck," he said, falling to his knees between my legs, his taut, muscular beauty outlined by another flash of distant lightning.

He fell onto all fours over me, caging my shoulders with his beefy, tree-trunk arms. "Are you wet?"

"Drenched," I whispered, laying back in the mud.

He pressed a hand over my pussy, fanning his fingers over mine, guiding my masturbation.

"You need to be wet for this."

He slid his slippery fingers up my equally slippery stomach in the cool, pounding rain. "You're so beautiful," he rasped, gliding his warm, rough hands everywhere, like he was slicking the rain all over me.

Finally, he stretched out over me.

"I have to be inside you hard."

That one didn't need an answer. I pulled him to me by his hair.

He rolled us over sideways. I shifted so that his body was perfectly flush to mine so that the most skin was touching, right down to the toes.

"God, you feel good," he said.

I felt his fingers move back to my hot, thrumming sex, sending delicious sensation deep into my core. He wasn't the only one on the edge.

"I have to..." he grated feverishly.

"Hurry," I said.

He slid a rough cheek over my nipple.

"After more of that," I said.

"Are you on any rocks or branches or anything? I don't want to fuck up your beautiful back," he said. "I don't want to drive you into something hard."

He didn't have to say any more. I knew he was so on the edge of control, he was worried that once he was in me, he wouldn't be able to stop. So he wanted to make sure nothing sharp was under me.

Like a fucking gentleman. A gentlemanly type of a bear.

"It's fine, Zeus. Fuck me into everything. Grind me down to China, I don't care. Just fill me. Please. Now."

He hissed out a breath and then he pushed my hand away from my crotch and guided himself into me, filling me.

"Yeah," I said as he stretched over me, cock swollen and huge inside me. "This."

He mumbled unintelligibly as he began to thrust.

"Harder," I said. "Fuck me senseless, Zeus."

He went harder. His wild fucking blotted out all the thoughts from my mind, all the fear and stalkers and weirdness. It was just me and Zeus and the biting rain and the cool, slippery mud, hurtling through the universe.

Uh-uh-uh, he grunted. *Uh-uh-uh.*

I caressed his back, feeling such love for him, wanting even more of him, whatever he had to give. The brutality, the care, the whole damn thing.

Uh-uh, he began. He mauled my jawline with his mouth as he fucked me. Like he wanted to eat my whole muddy, rain-soaked head.

Then he found my ear.

He bit down on my earlobe—hard.

The sharp, dark pleasure of it shot through me like a bullet, and I pulled him to me, trying to grab a hold on his slippery back.

"Yes," I panted. "More. Just...*fuck*..."

As if he could fuck me more.

My words didn't have to make sense. They were more like musical notes that I had to get out of myself or I'd burst.

Twin sensations warred for attention within me—the sting of his teeth on my earlobe and the building pleasure between my legs from the wild, huge thickness of him. Over and over, he invaded me with his massive girth, keeping hold of my ear with his teeth, merciless with the pain and pleasure under the dark, drenched sky.

I kind of didn't know where we were or what anything was. And suddenly my body came apart in a wild orgasm.

"Uh..." Zeus made a strangled noise. "*Uh-uh-uh*." He thrust once again, harder, grinding into me, which set off new waves of pleasure. I could feel the vibrations of his cock as he came and the warmth of his cum inside me.

The moment slid on and on under the pounding rain.

"Oh," I said, boneless beneath him. "Fuck."

I looked over then and saw a bobbing flashlight.

"Uh oh," I said.

Was it an interloper?

Somebody dangerous?

Zeus looked over and grunted. "One of us," he said.

"How can you tell?"

"From the shape."

Sure enough, it was Thor, playing the flashlight over our naked bodies. It was a little invasive. Like we were on display. Caught. Revealed.

Needless to say, it was hot.

"I brought a towel," Thor said. "Though you might be past where a towel can help. You guys are covered in mud."

Zeus rolled off of me and propped his head on his hand, slicking his hand over my wet belly. "Why didn't you come and join in?"

"I didn't think it was that kind of fuck," Thor said.

"Fuck her now," Zeus said.

"Yeah. *Thor—*" I wanted him to be in the mud with us, and to feel as good as we did. "Come here."

"We have to get back," Thor said.

"It's three in the morning," Zeus said. "The man's not going anywhere."

"It's four," Thor said.

"Man's still not going anywhere."

"Come here," I said. "I want to touch you in the mud. Let me lick the rain off you."

"We don't serially fuck you," Thor said. "That's for a prostitute, being serially fucked."

"Isis wants you to come down here," Zeus said.

"No," Thor said.

"It's amazing in the rain and mud," I said. "You would like it."

"That's not how it works," Thor said.

"I never heard of any no-serial-fucking rule," I said.

In truth, we never did it where I fucked one guy after another. But right at that moment, it seemed sort of dirty in a way that I liked.

"I want you to fuck me serially," I said, heat pooling in my belly. "I want you to fuck me while Zeus watches."

"We don't pass you around," Thor said again.

"If it's what Ice wants, it's what Ice gets," Zeus said.

"Come here, Isis," Thor said. "The towel's still partly dry. We'll dry you off and get you back in the truck."

Zeus stood, glorious and naked. "Ice wants you to come down there."

Distant lightning illuminated his pale ass as he got up into Thor's face.

I thought he might kiss Thor, but instead he drew a finger down his cheek, trailing a line of mud like war paint.

Thor glared, chest rising and falling beneath the rain-soaked T-shirt that hugged his muscles.

One more inch and they'd be kissing. My bank robbers never kissed each other—the only kind of sexual contact they had with each other was when they were fucking me, and that was more incidental. But I liked to imagine them kissing.

The rain pounded harder, louder.

"You know you want to fuck her," Zeus said. "You know you want to."

Thor watched Zeus's eyes. Pulses of lighting flashed on the horizon, illuminating his mud-streaked face and ferocious expression and wet blond hair.

He was a hot, beautiful Visigoth. Hot, beautiful, and massively hard.

And I wanted him like mad.

Zeus raised his other hand and swiped that one down Thor's other cheek, so that Thor had fat mud stripes on both cheeks. A kind of weird challenge. The mud stripes made his cheekbones even more pronounced.

Thor pushed Zeus away. "Fuck off. I'm not fucking Isis serially. It's not fun for her."

He came to me and knelt, holding the towel.

I sat up. "It would be fun for me tonight."

He wrapped the towel around my shoulders. The warmth felt good, but I wanted it to be his body, not some towel.

Zeus muscled in beside Thor. "I'll hold her and bite her ear while you fuck her," Zeus said. "She'll love that."

My pulse was racing, imagining him holding me, imagining his meaty hands on my body while Thor fucked me.

"No fucking you serially. Zeus, you go find your clothes."

"What is with you?" Zeus took the towel from Thor. "I fucked her, I'll clean her up."

"Fuck you." Thor grabbed the other end of the towel. I jumped away as they struggled over the towel, collapsing into the mud, wrestling over it.

"You guys!" I said. "Stop it! What the hell?" I didn't know how to feel about my guys wrestling and rolling in the mud.

Until I realized it was the hottest thing ever.

They rolled around like wild animals, coming to a stop only when they hit the base of the tree. Thor was on top of Zeus, then Zeus was on top of Thor. I went over and shoved at Zeus's back with my foot. "Hey!"

Thor hooked his leg in Zeus's leg and flipped them over so that Thor was on top.

Zeus grunted and pressed a palm into Thor's muddy chest.

That was enough. I got down there with them and grabbed Thor's slippery shoulders, trying to pull him off Zeus. No go.

"Hey," I said, trying to push Thor since pulling didn't work. Then I just pressed my weight onto him. They'd stopped fighting now that I was there, so I kept on horning in, pushing my way between the panting guys, exploiting the fact that they wouldn't hurt me. I felt Zeus's hands on my shoulders, gripping me and positioning me firmly on top of himself...and almost under Thor.

I grabbed Thor's shoulders and started kissing him.

Thor gusted out a breath and closed his fists around my hair, kissing me back, holding my head in place.

He angled his head, forcing my mouth open with his tongue, shoving it in.

I pulled him to me more tightly.

I could feel Zeus's hands around my shoulders, locking me between them.

I pressed my hands to Thor's cheeks and pushed his face from mine, staring into his eyes. "Fuck me serially," I said. "Use me."

"Ice." He slid his hands along my breasts. I wrapped my legs around him. His pants fabric felt rough against my tender folds.

"Come here." Zeus pulled me backwards onto his lap. He was sitting back against the tree, I realized.

Thor came with us, kneeling between my legs. He leaned in and slid his hands all over my breasts, then he bent in, licking the rain, and hell, maybe the mud. "God, Isis. You're wet and dirty and so hot."

"All the better for you to fuck me," I gasped.

He leaned in for a kiss, pinching my nipples lightly, teasing me like I liked. Zeus pressed his strong, firm hands into my belly, holding me flush to him.

"Take off your pants, Thor," Zeus said. "You have one second before I start biting her ear. She needs you to be fucking her while I bite her ear."

"Hurry," I said.

Thor stood, working his belt.

Zeus closed his lips over my ear in the spot where he'd bit me before. I braced myself for the dark pain of it as he held me to him. He pushed his hands down my belly to my sex, or more the tops of my thighs, spreading my legs apart for Thor, and then he slid his hands back between my legs, but he stopped before touching me at my thrumming core. He simply pressed down on either side.

Delicious sensation flooded my core as he compressed my pussy. "Oh, yeah," I said. All the nerve endings in my clit felt plumped up, exposed, ready, tingly.

I needed even more desperately to be touched, to be fucked directly. "Do you like this?" he grated into my ear.

"Yes," I panted.

Thor's cock jutted out like a feral, blunt rod, briefly strobed by the lightning flashes on the horizon.

"Keep doing it," I said. "Do it while Thor fucks me."

Thor fell to his knees in front of me. "You heard the lady," Thor said, rubbing his cock on my plumped out clit.

Oh, this was a new move. And it was brilliant.

Thor kissed me, fucking me with his tongue. I grabbed his cock and pressed it to my sex between Zeus's merciless hands. Waves of mad pleasure rolled over me. I felt his cock jump in my grip. He was as on the verge as I was. I pressed it into my center. He slid in easily with a deep groan.

"I always want you to fuck me," I whispered. "Always." Well, that wasn't exactly true—there were times I wasn't in the mood—but at the moment, I couldn't imagine a time like that. It seemed impossible to not want this delicious feeling, to not want these hands on me, to not want my bank robbers to take their pleasure in my body. Especially with Zeus's hands down there, pushing my sensitized lips flush against Thor's grinding cock.

I threw my head back to rest on Zeus's shoulder. He turned his head and bit my earlobe. "Ah!" I said in surprise. With all the action down there, I'd forgotten he meant to bite my ear. "Ah!"

I arched my back, lost in the wild feeling.

This seemed to excite Thor, because he thrust harder, which increased the intensity of the friction, and I broke apart, launching into a mind-numbing orgasm that spun through me. "Oh, yes," I said as Thor came with a cry, thrusting in one last time, then stilling.

The rain pounded as I lay there, strung out between my guys.

Thor leaned his forehead into my neck. "Fuck," he whispered as the tremors moved through him. He rolled off.

"*Uh-uh-uh,*" Zeus panted. I realized vaguely that he'd taken one of his hands off me, and that he was doing himself.

I turned around and knocked his hand away, gripping his slick cock in my own hand, then I bent over and took him in my mouth and sucked and stroked in the way that most drives him wild.

I felt Zeus's hand come over the back of my head. "Goddess," he rasped, pushing my head down over his huge rod. His whole body tightened as he came into my mouth with a strangled cry, cock pulsating between my lips, on and on.

"Wow," I said, collapsing back onto him.

"Sheesh, I didn't think I'd come again," he said.

"I didn't think I'd come again," I said.

Thor lay on his side next to us, head propped up on his hand. He pressed his lips to my shoulder. "So much for the clean, dry towel."

I smoothed his hair back so he looked like a 1920s guy. "You will never make me feel used, or like a prostitute," I said. "I always want you to do everything you want."

Thor kissed my ear and whispered, "Except sometimes when you wake up crabby."

"Yeah. There's that."

He stood up. "We need to go." He put out his hand. I took it and let him pull me up. Then I reached back for Zeus. He took my hand and stood.

The tension level between the three of us had dropped from eleven to one now that we'd fucked our brains out.

Thor picked up the muddy towel. "I don't know why Odin sent me out here with the towel. We should've waited for you to come to the vehicle."

"Odin sent you out with a towel?" I asked.

"Yeah," Thor said. "It seemed like a good idea at the time."

I squinted. It wasn't a good idea at all. Like Thor said, the towel would've stayed dry if they'd waited for us to return.

Unless the towel staying dry wasn't the point.

My clothes lay nearby, only slightly damaged. Zeus's clothes were scattered all over. We helped him find them and wrung them out best we could. Then we headed back to the SUV. Even from far off, I could see Odin in there, face lit by the glow of his phone.

It was then that it came to me that Odin had engineered all of this. He'd decided we needed to have sex to feel saner. He'd made it happen. And now I was less worried, Zeus was less primal, and Thor was less distracted.

Had Odin been quietly controlling things all along? Or was I looking at a power shift? I'd always thought of Zeus as the leader of the group. Was I wrong on that? Was Odin the power behind the power? Or did Odin only take over when Zeus was wildly emotional?

Zeus got to the vehicle first and pulled open the door. "Tell me we have more clothes in here."

Odin looked us over with an exaggerated frown of disgust. "You *ripped* Isis's shirt?"

I smiled.

Zeus snorted. "I ripped mine. She ripped hers."

Odin slanted his eyes at the back of the vehicle. "All we have is one old sweatshirt. Isis gets it. Maybe a few other towels."

We were back on the road two minutes later with Zeus driving. Thor and Zeus and I had towels to sit on, but we were still pretty wet and muddy. I pulled the sweatshirt over my head, grateful for the warmth.

"This guy's place is about fifteen more minutes out," Odin said. "Zeus, what happens if we want to take our time with him? What happens if you call in sick to the HVAC crew? Are we screwed?"

Zeus thought it would be fine just once. They needed him now. No way would they fire him.

I looked over at Zeus, who was wiping his face with his hand, but it only smeared around the mud. Same with Thor. It was a freaky look they had going. "We need to wash up properly and find new clothes," I said.

Odin eyed me in the rearview mirror. His look was just a little too sparkly. "Do we?"

I straightened when I got it—he wanted us to go question this guy looking like scary freaks.

I studied his face, even after he looked back at the road. Odin was all calm, confident determination, revealing nothing.

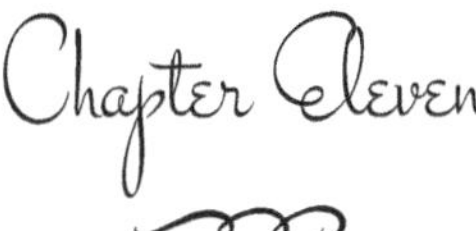

THE GIGIS HAD ONCE POINTED OUT THAT MY GUYS chose the most difficult and dangerous form of robbery to specialize in—bank takeovers.

There was always a lot of yelling and screaming during our robberies, and lots of problems always cropped up that we had to fix on the fly.

I never really appreciated what masterful criminals they were until I saw them do a truly easy crime: entering Ingvey's little matchbox house, a mini 1950s home on a block of mini 1950s homes.

They blew in there like it was nothing.

This entire investigation was making me see things a little differently.

My guys could be robbing mansions in their sleep. Running sophisticated con games without a thought. Hell, they could probably have started five different companies and made five different fortunes by now, but scary takeover robberies was what hurt ZOX the most.

So that's what they did.

It was amazing—and incredibly sad, too.

So Odin and Zeus glided in like flash ninjas, guns drawn, splitting up and becoming invisible while Thor and I waited inside the dark foyer.

"Okay, come on," Thor whispered, responding to a signal I neither saw nor heard. He went in, also with his gun drawn, keeping me behind him. Thor was playing defense.

Zeus appeared out of nowhere and pointed at a spot in the darkest corner of the kitchen. I waited there while the three of them did whatever they did. The walls of the kitchen and dining room beyond were lit by streetlights outside.

Judging by the photography, Ingvey was very into architecture.

Muffled exclamations sounded from the dark hallway. Moments later, Zeus and Odin were hauling a sleepy-looking man into the living room.

Ingvey wore boxers and a T-shirt. His long brown hair was mussed and messy, and he was trembling visibly. "I didn't do anything," Ingvey protested as Zeus and Odin parked him at the head of the kitchen table.

"You know her?" Odin asked him. "You recognize this woman?"

Ingvey regarded me, wide-eyed, like I was going to attack him or something. "Am I supposed to?"

Zeus grabbed his hair, as if to point his head more firmly in my direction. "Answer the question."

The man cringed. "No!"

I felt sorry for him. What if he wasn't the guy?

"You fucked up when you threatened her," Zeus growled.

Ingvey looked bewildered.

Odin put a hand on Zeus's shoulder. "I've got it."

Zeus let go, and Odin took the chair next to him. "What about the package?" Odin asked. "We know it's you."

"I don't know what you're talking about." Ingvey turned and addressed me. "Do I know you?"

"You don't talk to her, you talk to us," Zeus said.

"Look at me," Odin said. Apparently they had a kind of good cop, bad cop thing going, or more a scary cop, less-scary cop thing. Odin rattled off questions. Ingvey answered as Zeus stormed off and started tearing through the house, opening drawers and dumping garbage. Either Ingvey was innocent, or he was doing a very good impersonation of a man completely bewildered by the situation.

And then the detail of his fingerprints on the shoebox came up. They were on the baggie, too.

"Well shit, I work at Giorgio's," Ingvey said. "The shoe store."

"You work at a shoe store?"

"I touch shoeboxes all day."

"How do you explain their presence on the plastic bag?"

"I don't know. I work in a store. I touch things all day."

Odin narrowed his eyes. Then he stormed out to the truck and came back in with the shoebox. "This from your store?"

"We have those. Or had them. Last year's model."

"You know this to be from your store?" Odin barked.

"May I?" Ingvey held out his hands. Odin let him take the shoebox and Ingvey lifted the lid. "You mind if I rip it?"

Zeus had returned. He and Odin exchanged glances.

"Go for it," Zeus said.

Ingvey pulled apart a corner of the lid. "Yup, it's ours."

"There's a tracker in there?" Odin asked.

"Anti-theft device. Other stores use this kind, but the way it's inserted, this one's probably ours."

"Can you tell us who bought this model?" Zeus asked.

As it turned out, he could—if the person had used a credit card. It would be a long list, he warned, and he'd have to get into work and get it off the computer. His shift didn't start until ten.

"We'll be in there at ten after ten, Odin promised, pulling a few bills out of his pocket and slapping them down on Ingvey's kitchen table. "That's for waking you up. There'll be more for the list. Okay? We good?"

Ingvey regarded him grimly.

"And if you have cops waiting for us, we'll know," growled Zeus.

"And you will feel the wrath of us beat down upon you like a thousand blazing fists, and we will crush you and this house," Odin added.

We used the interim to grab dry clothes from a nearby department store and clean up. Thor called Matteo, who reluctantly agreed to sit on the bank for our shift even though he'd said he wouldn't.

We were parked across the street and down a ways from the shoe store by 9:30. My guys thought it was unlikely Ingvey would have cops waiting for us, but they wanted to check. I certainly thought it was unlikely after Zeus's manhandling and Odin's thousand-blazing-fists threats—one of his more colorful ones of late.

Odin and Zeus were sure it wasn't Ingvey at this point. Zeus had a theory that the culprit had given Ingvey the plastic bag to touch during some transaction.

Odin peered through binoculars. Fifteen minutes later, Ingvey met an older woman at the shoe store door. "He looks nervous. Don't see cops. They're going in."

At ten after ten, Odin went in. Five minutes later, he came back out and crossed the street with a shopping bag. He swung into the passenger seat. "Got it."

Zeus peeled out.

Odin handed the bag back. "A gift for you," he said.

A shoebox was inside. "Thanks," I said.

"You got a name?" Thor asked.

"More like a hundred," Odin grumbled. "That's as far as he could narrow it. The box he used was from a *fucking-g* popular brand."

"Can I open it?" I asked.

"Please," Odin said.

I pulled off the lid of the shoebox. Inside a nest of white tissue paper lay bejeweled, pink high heels. "These are like candy," I said. "In a good way."

"We'll always take care of you," Odin said.

I smiled. "Thank you."

"And now maybe you'll stop disrespecting the tattoo with unkempt feet," Odin said.

I snorted.

"Her feet are awesome," Zeus said, merging onto the highway. He was unhappy with the length of the list. The stalker definitely upset my guys more than he upset me.

Odin split the list with Thor, and they began to vet the names on their smartphones, knocking out the females, the out-of-state buyers, and buyers under the age of eighteen and over the age of sixty. Thor gave Odin his list and Odin narrowed down the people more from their Facebook pages.

"Seriously?" I said. "You're ruling out people by their Facebook pages?"

"Best OSINT ever," Odin said, thumbs flying over his keypad. Open-source intelligence, he meant. They'd used the term before. I couldn't remember what the NT was.

By the time we were ten minutes from home, Odin had the list narrowed down to five. And at the top was one T. Hansen, a.k.a. Travis Hansen. Or in Thor's words, Sleazy Travis Hansen.

Apparently everybody in their set knew Sleazy Travis, though the man hadn't shown his face lately because there was a warrant out for his arrest. He'd been locked up twice for sexual assault, and he had jumped bail on rape charges. He was known for stalking his victims, including leaving strange gifts.

"Travis dies," Zeus grumbled.

"If we can find him," Thor said. "He might not even be in town."

He and Zeus discussed the way they'd work the grapevine. The problem, apparently, wasn't whether they'd learn where he was holed up, it was whether they could learn where he was holed up without his knowing they were after him.

"Because then he'll really disappear," Odin said. "Hiding from the cops is a lot easier than hiding from us."

I didn't doubt it.

Zeus pulled off at a gas station and Thor took over driving on the next leg. I sat on the passenger side while Odin and Zeus worked the phones in the back seat, conferring and beating the bushes for Travis, going hard at some people, soft at others.

We grabbed gourmet breakfast sandwiches at a place near downtown, then made stops at two bars and one apartment building—both times Thor and I had to wait in the SUV. Both times Odin and Zeus came out looking a little more mussed than when they went in.

After the last stop, we had an address. Travis was staying in the shed behind his mother's house.

"The cops couldn't find him?" Odin spat out. "At the mother's house? It's Sex Offender 101. The mother's house." He seemed almost annoyed.

"Matter of time now," Zeus said to me, low and hard. "We protect our own, goddess."

Shivers ran over me.

We parked on the far end of the street. Zeus and Odin slipped out and melted into the neighborhood. Thor and I were to keep watch at the front with the motor running, just in case.

Thor checked his email again.

"Any news?" I asked.

"No," he said. "The midwives still hope they can turn the baby."

"She's lucky to have you," I said.

"I should be down there," he said.

"You can't just sit there. You said yourself it could be weeks before she goes into labor."

"Yeah," he said.

"You're just two hours away," I pointed out. A little more, actually, especially if it was rush hour. "And the midwives are there. Don't they know what they're doing?"

"They're the best, but neither of them has delivered a breech as risky as this one. Well, one of them has, but it went badly, which is worse than no experience."

A car came up the street behind us. The driver, a lone man, matched Travis's description—somewhat.

Thor slid down in his seat, watching the side mirror. "Too old."

Zeus called and Thor put it on speaker. Travis wasn't there, but they'd found evidence in the shed. Definitely him.

"Damn." Thor clicked off. "How are you doing? You don't seem freaked out."

"I was at first, but I know this will be okay. I wish he was there, but hey, of all the people who have threats against them in the world, I think I'm the safest."

"I'd say you're safer than the president." He gazed out at the street, scanning a new car coming down the way. A woman. "It's hard to believe that anybody would decide to go after you. It's like poking a hornet's nest, but then again, people do stupid things. And sometimes people have a death wish."

Chapter Twelve

Ten minutes later, Zeus and Odin were bounding back through the neighborhood with clear evidence bags. One seemed to contain white butcher paper; the other held what looked like gloves.

Thor and I got out and schlepped into the back seat.

Zeus flung open the driver's side door. "Not there. But it's him."

"*Looks* like him," Odin corrected, getting in the passenger side. "Still circumstantial."

"We'll know when we see him face-to-face." Zeus shut the door quietly. "That shed is completely wired up with cameras. Almost as secure as our hideout, and he dug a lower level. The place is so empty and clean, you almost couldn't tell somebody was living there."

"Clean?" Thor asked.

"The man is a neat freak," Odin said. "Pathologically neat. The mother's house is even worse. She has plastic over all the furniture."

"Even the kitchen table," Zeus said. "The lamps. Disposable plates and utensils. Who lives like that?"

"The mentally ill, typically," Odin said. "Maybe she tried to keep plastic on the son in a metaphorical sense—keep him pristine. Sexual predators like Travis often have issues around mothers and bodily functions."

"Yikes," I said as a white car passed.

"I wonder who wired the shed for him," Odin continued, snapping on his seatbelt. "Manning? Not a lot of guys will wire up a shed like that and keep their mouth shut. We found all that butcher paper in their dumpster. If we laid it out next to the butcher paper from the package with the feather, pieces would line up. I bet you anything."

Just then, Zeus peeled out.

"Hey—"

"That was him." Zeus took a corner and the white car ahead squealed around another. "Gotcha."

"Take it easy," Thor cautioned as the driver of the white car started getting more erratic.

"Travis knew, goddammit," Zeus said. "Somebody tipped him. He should've been in there."

We sped after him onto a crowded surface street. Travis wove in and out through a pack of cars.

"Slow down," Thor said. "He's gonna kill someone."

Travis went through a stoplight, nearly causing a crash. That's when the sirens started.

"Damn!" Odin said. "Hang back."

We slowed, moving in behind a cop car. Two more cop cars came in from the side to join the first. Zeus slowed to the speed limit. The chase got farther ahead, and soon the cherry-red lights disappeared.

Odin fired up his police scanner app. "They're taking Bentham Road. Go west on 28th."

Zeus did a U-turn and took 28th, going on to follow Odin's ever-changing directions. We turned left and right and left.

A helicopter sounded overhead.

"Do you think they know who they have?" I asked.

"Could be," Zeus said.

"Hold on," Odin said as the voices through the radio got frenetic. "Shit. He crashed."

"Bad?" Thor asked.

Odin shook his head. "Unknown. Zeus, turn up here. Here—this light." He directed us to the crash site.

It took a while to get there because the crash had slowed traffic in both directions. Red lights lit up the palm trees and houses. By the time we neared, they were loading Travis into an ambulance and we saw only a flash of him, all bloody and twisted. They were waving people past.

"Did you see him, Thor?" Zeus asked. "What do you think?"

"Doesn't look good," Thor said. "From the look of his car, he's lucky he's not dead."

"He preferred to risk death and arrest," Odin said.

I finished his sentence in my mind: *He preferred to risk death and arrest over dealing with the God Pack.*

We arrived home exhausted and dirty. Matteo called to say that things had gone as usual. It was nearly closing time.

Thor called the hospital and finagled an update on Travis. Critical but stable.

I was surprised to see Odin and Zeus, both wearing latex gloves, smoothing out the crumpled butcher paper from Travis's garbage. They had the paper from the feather package already laid out to compare to this new evidence.

Zeus looked up and caught my eye. "Just to be sure," he said. "You know how thorough we like to be."

I smiled. Such professionals. It was a little bit sad, to think of all the things they could've been. The work they'd done back in the agency had probably saved countless lives.

"What's that look?" Zeus barked.

"No look," I said.

"Go meet us in the hot tub," Odin said, not looking up.

I headed for my room instead and took a shower. When I got out to our back porch, my guys were already in the tub, which made a peanut-shaped hole in our wood-slat deck. You could see the setting sun glinting through the trees all around us.

"What took you so long?" Thor asked, sliding all the way down. The tips of his longish blond hair grazed the water.

I undid the belt to my fluffy robe, swishing my toe in the warm water. "Girls take longer with everything." I peeled off the robe and stepped into the delicious and bubbly warmth.

Zeus snorted.

"But it's always worth the wait," I added as I sunk down next to Thor. *Heaven.*

"I'm glad you're safe," Thor said, sliding an arm over my shoulders. "No blood on our hands. We didn't have to carry out vigilante justice. Travis is on his third strike, so he'll stay inside."

"I want to visit him," Zeus announced.

"Are you afraid he'll tell the authorities about us?" I asked.

Zeus sniffed, like that was the craziest thing he'd ever heard. "Sleazy Travis would never snitch on us. We could get to him so fast."

"What is it, then?" Thor asked.

Zeus paused, as though his thoughts were baffling even him. "Just to make sure it's really him in that hospital bed. And I want to ask him to his face about the package he left. I want you to come too, Odin."

"He won't admit it," Odin said.

"I know, but did you think it was too easy?" Zeus asked. "Did it feel too easy?"

"Hmm," Odin said, considering it

Zeus grunted.

"You're not suggesting we postpone the Prime because we're awesome in ferreting out our enemies, are you?" Thor asked.

"It felt easy. And the frame job on Ingvey—that was off," Zeus said, ever the instinctual one. His gaze fell to me. "It can't hurt to make sure. It felt so easy."

"So easy for *us*, you mean. Easy relative to the shit we do now," Odin said. "Running down criminals is much easier than knocking off the most *fucking-g* well-protected structures in the Western hemisphere." Odin flicked water at Zeus. "You, my friend, are unused to easy work."

"Why *can't* it be easy?" I asked. "Why can't that be a goal? Don't you guys deserve better?"

Thor groaned. "Is this the Tunisian island again?"

"It's being good to yourselves," I said. "You've messed with your enemies, but where does it end?"

Odin frowned.

"She's picked out an island for us to retire on," Thor explained.

Zeus furrowed his brow. "You knew this was what you were signing on for when you joined us, Isis," he said, seeming troubled. "Are you regretting—"

"No! Of course not," I said. "I wouldn't go back and change a thing. I'm with you one hundred percent, you know that."

"It's our moral obligation to *fucking-g* make them wish we were dead, Isis. What possible reason would we have to abandon it?" Odin stared into the dark trees.

"Because you need to start being good to yourselves," I said.

Because I love you, I thought.

I needed to tell them how much I loved them—each of them individually, and them together—but not in the middle of an argument.

I knew they loved each other, too. They thought they were saying it with their matching tattoos, but it wasn't the same thing. Especially now that they'd soon be emblazoning that stupid *You WISH we were dead, motherfuckers* motto on our arms. That wasn't about love.

"We can't just fade away and let them win," Zeus said.

"Haven't you ever heard? Living well is the best revenge."

Odin shook his head.

I thought again about their talents and intelligence. What they'd given up. It made me feel desperately sad—too sad to sit there one second longer.

I wanted, suddenly, to be alone. To mourn the happiness they could've had. Could still have.

"Excuse me for wanting some peace and serenity for you." I shot up out of the tub, grabbed a towel, and headed toward the sliding door.

Stupid me thinking I could walk away from an argument with my stubborn guys. Heavy footfalls shook the wooden slats of the porch behind me; heavy hands grabbed me and picked me up.

I tried to wriggle out of Zeus's arms, but he had me. "Screw you, I'm not going back in the tub."

"No choice," Zeus said, climbing back down into the hot water. He settled me on his lap and held me there, arms like a vice.

Odin's gaze was sharp. "We will have peace and happiness *and* we will have vengeance. We take what we want, Isis. And we are not going to fade away in some retirement paradise, fishing like old men. You don't want that life any more than we do. You of all people don't want a life without thrills."

"What about the thrills of making your own meaning? Remember what Matteo said at Guvvey's? If you spend your life reacting to somebody, they control you as much as if you spend your life obeying them."

"That's not what he said," Odin said. "You added something."

"Giving ZOX pain is the opposite of obeying them," Zeus said. "We're doing the Prime next week."

Odin swished his foot, brown toes forming a knobby fin, moving through the water. "You may not agree with that decision, but if you're participating, we need you committed—one hundred percent there. Are you there or not? That's the question on the table right now."

"Of course I'm there, a hundred percent."

"He's right. We need you there fully," Zeus said, keeping his massive arms around me, a prison and a cocoon. "It's okay if you're not. I'm sure we could find somebody to fill in if you're feeling apprehensive. We can't go in with you half into it, that's the thing. This is the Prime. We could get Bentley to drive. One of the Gigi's would drive if they knew we were hitting it."

My belly nearly sunk through the floor of the tub. "You see me as interchangeable with Bentley or the Gigis?"

"Of course not," Thor said quickly. "Never!"

"That's what it sounded like!"

"You could never be replaced," Thor said.

"Bentley and the Gigis are pros, that's all," Zeus said, warm in my ear. "So you wouldn't have to feel bad if you didn't want to—"

"I don't need Bentley or one of the Gigis filling in for me!" I wriggled out of Zeus's hold and he finally let me go. "I'm all in," I said, trying to keep my voice calm, but it hurt that he'd even suggested it. "I just think *live for vengeance* is a shitty long-term strategy, that's all."

Odin gave me a look I couldn't read. In our normal life, my current attitude might merit some erotic punishment. The fact that it was off the table showed the seriousness of this conversation.

"I'm always in," I added. "And other people don't have half the allegiance to you guys that I do. I can't believe you would suggest it—"

"He was just giving you an out," Thor said.

"I don't need an out. I'd tell you if I wasn't into playing my role a hundred percent. I need you guys to trust I'd speak up on that."

"We trust you, goddess," Zeus said.

"Maybe not, if you think I'd endanger you by being half-ass on a heist. You guys look out for me, but this thing goes both ways. Let me look out for you."

Odin came to me through the water and pressed a warm, wet hand to my cheek. "You were trying to talk us into quitting, goddess," he whispered. "You know what that feels like? It feels like *you* want to quit."

Finally I understood.

I'd scared them.

"I never want to quit." I put my hand over his, sandwiching it onto my cheek, wondering suddenly if Venus had tried to get them to quit. I know she'd messed up a robbery shortly before her suicide. "I don't want to quit, I swear. I love our life," I said, remembering the day I got the cloud and lightning tattoo to match theirs. How it made us a family. Us as the four bolts coming out of the cloud. How proud I felt.

Odin trailed his hand down my slick shoulder. "Our commitment to each other is how we survive as a pack."

"I know," I said. It was how they knew they'd always go back for each other. How they knew they could count on each other. Odin didn't use the word *pack* lightly. They were like the human version of a werewolf pack from the books I loved, fighting to the death for each other. "Talking about the island, that isn't me pulling away. It's me thinking about Travis on that stretcher today and hating that it could be one of you someday. It's me wanting to be with you forever, no matter what. I'm with you on everything. Always."

"Goddess," Zeus said, turning my head and kissing me.

Out the corner of my eye, I saw Odin float back to his spot in the tub. He seemed unconvinced.

Thor squeezed in next to me, resting a hand on my thigh under the water.

"And you'll get the tattoo?" Odin asked.

"Of course," I said, even though the idea of those negative words on my skin bothered me.

Maybe I could still at least talk them out of that. Or find something better for the tattoo to say, something positive and badass. There was still time.

Odin's wet hair shone like obsidian in the moonlight. "*You WISH we were dead, motherfuckers.*" He watched my eyes. "It's time to finish them. This week."

"I'm in," I said smoothly.

The heist was a few days off, and there was a lot to do yet.

Surely he wouldn't want to spend time on lengthy tattooing sessions.

His eyes glittered in dark.

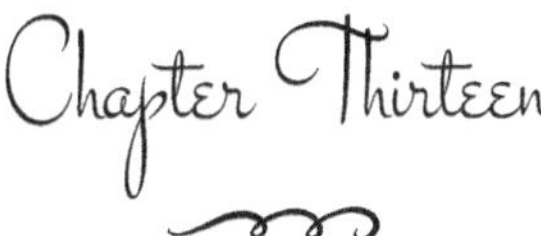

Chapter Thirteen

Odin and Thor and I were sitting outside the bank two days later, squished together in the front seat, when Thor's phone rang.

"Yeah?"

The caller had a lot to say, rambling on and on. You could hear his tone, but not the words. Thor thanked him and told him he'd courier over some money, and then he cut the connection.

"That was our panther guy from the university with the results on the feather."

The feather was over seventy years old, apparently, and from an eagle. The panther guy and his colleagues thought that it might be from an old taxidermy piece, judging from the dust and dirt pattern.

"That's weird," Odin said.

"What's weird?" Thor asked.

"There was no taxidermy in Travis's place. Or his mother's."

"Maybe it was there and you didn't see it," Thor said.

"No, there *wouldn't* be any," Odin said. "Ever. All the dirt and dust? Those two wouldn't let a stuffed eagle within a hundred feet of their door."

Thor grumbled.

Odin swore under his breath.

Zeus and Odin had paid a visit to Travis in the prison hospital the night before.

Travis had denied being the stalker, but Zeus and Odin had expected him to deny it. I'd asked them if they were convinced. *"He was drugged up,"* Zeus had said simply.

Odin hadn't liked it. *"You can see so little in a drugged man's eyes,"* he'd said. But the circumstantial evidence was there. The paper was in his dumpster. He bought the shoes. He'd done that type of crime in the past.

Odin stared out at the bank steps. It was nearly eleven, almost time again for my deposit.

"On one hand, it makes no sense he'd use such a dirty object when he's practically germaphobic, judging from the many hand sanitizers. But I could make a case for it."

"Like what?" I asked.

"That he keeps a *fucking-g* vice grip of sterility over his home and thoughts, that he associates functions of the body, and in particular anything sexual, with dirt and sin. Therefore, he would seek out something horribly besmirched as a gift to you."

"And as we know, there's no better way to a girl's heart than a horribly besmirched gift," I said.

"Or else it wasn't him," Thor said.

"We didn't get a confession, it's true," Odin said. "But in any investigative work, unlike police shows, it typically *is* the obvious that is the solution. And since he's been inside, Isis hasn't had any contact from her stalker. There were two communications from the stalker within twenty-four hours, but nothing for two days now. That's a clue in and of itself."

"Should we wait to be sure?" Thor asked. "Considering how soon..." *How soon we hit the Prime.* He didn't have to finish that sentence. We were eating, breathing, and sleeping the Prime.

Odin watched a pair of blonde women in pink track suits cross the road. He considered this for some time.

"When I was a boy," Odin said, "my brother and I used to fish in this lake in the High Atlas Mountains. Right off the shore." He described the color of the water, the smell of the air, the fishing poles he and his brother had made.

I glanced at Thor. His face was perfectly neutral, but I suspected he was just as surprised as I was.

And not only about Morocco having lakes.

Odin never talked about his childhood. Zeus and Thor had figured out that Odin's mother was mentally ill and his father had left, but nothing much beyond it. Odin's using the term *my family* made me think this story could be from before his father had left.

"My brother and I dipped our lines into a patch of dark water and waited," he said. "But then we heard the loud splash of a massive fish jumping some thirty paces down the shore. We pulled out our lines and ran to that spot and put in our lines to fish there. Soon after, we heard a large fish, perhaps the same, jump in the water near where we had first been. We pulled out our lines and ran back to our original spot and fished there, hoping to catch this fish. And then it happened again. The sound of a fish, jumping in the new spot. We were running back and forth like fools."

"Somebody throwing rocks," I guessed.

Odin regarded the bank with a dark look. "My *mother* throwing rocks. Making fools of us. We didn't realize it until we heard her screeching with laughter."

"That's mean," I said.

"Not at all," Odin said. "It was one of the few valuable lessons she taught us. Proceed with confidence. Know that you chose the path you chose for a reason. Don't let the plunk of stones down the shoreline distract you, or you will forever be running back and forth like fools."

Thor and I sat silently. Sure, okay, it was a good thing to bear in mind, not to chase willy nilly after every passing notion, but it seemed a horrible thing for a mother to do. And then laugh.

"This taxidermy information. Perhaps it is a stone," Odin said quietly.

"I don't know," I said.

He turned back to meet my eyes. "An island in Tunisia. That is a stone."

"You made your point on that," I said.

"Did I?" he asked.

I gave him a look. "I need to do my deposit," I said, gathering my things. I slipped out the back and onto the sunny sidewalk.

Making a bank deposit is far easier when you don't have vibrating implements along for the ride.

Less fun, but much easier. I guess this made me the horse running on dry land now.

I went in and out as I had on so many days, wearing my wig of fabulous long blonde hair with a fabulous outfit.

The fifteen-minute window was still as soft as ever.

The guard flirted with the far-end teller.

The desk clerks checked their phones, and everything loosened up as soon as the evil overlord took his break.

I thought angrily of my old bank boss, an unfortunate cross between a gross perv and a greedy megalomaniac, but I realized I should be thankful for him. If he'd been a nice boss, maybe I would've tried to defend the bank instead of helping the robbers.

Sure, I didn't like that the Prime Royale would be so difficult and possibly dangerous, and I definitely didn't like this new tattoo idea as much as I did at first, but I loved how they defied the entire world, how they lived large in spite of all the odds being aligned against them.

I loved them, that was the truth of it.

My guys needed me, and I would do anything for them.

I stepped through the open doors, past the doormen, and out into the sunshine, feeling suddenly hopeful. My guys were intensely fixated on vengeance, but maybe pulling off a robbery of the Prime would quench it, like a big glass of bank robber lemonade hitting a parched throat. The Prime was the ultimate prize, after all. Unless you counted something like Fort Knox.

Needless to say, I wouldn't be mentioning *that* to my guys!

The rest of the stakeout went like clockwork. And Lupe, our expectant mother and criminal sister in Santa Rosa, was feeling good. The midwives hadn't turned the baby, but she was doing well otherwise. Everything was looking up. Odin was even talking about playing chess later, which made me think that maybe he'd abandoned his plans to complete our non-life-positive tattoos.

Wishful thinking, as it turned out.

That evening, Thor and Zeus took off to grab takeout and champagne for our two-nights-before-a job celebration.

A few minutes later, Odin strolled into the kitchen where I was clicking through the Farfetch site.

One of the great things about being in a bank robbing gang is that you can afford designer outfits—the real ones, not the knockoffs.

"Tattoo time," he said.

"You're finishing it *now*?" I asked.

He smiled his beautiful and dangerous smile. "You have a problem with that?" He came and spun me around on my stool, standing between my legs.

I had a problem all right—with a tattoo like a curse. But at the end of the day, if my guys were getting it, I wanted it. Showing that I was a true part of the gang was more important than the specifics of some tattoo.

He kissed my neck. "Are you ready?"

"Sure am," I whispered, reaching down and pressing my hand to his cock, hoping to bypass his mind by communicating directly with his libido. I wrapped my fingers almost all the way around it in a way that I hoped was saying, *Can't you think of something better to do?*

He removed my hand. "Go sit on the couch, goddess."

Sigh.

I cast around for a delaying idea, but without sex, my bag of tricks was pretty empty.

And, after long hours of getting the angel holding the scrolls, I was used to sitting still for the painful little needles without being tied down, so I didn't need erotic distraction. "Timing seems a bit much."

He spoke close to my face. "I want us to have them complete for the Prime."

"You mean to finish them all tonight?"

"And tomorrow. As much as I can." He pulled me gently to him, kissing me. My heartbeat kicked into double-time as he pushed his tongue into my mouth, body hard and good up against mine, and the swivel stool was just the right height.

"I'm ready to start the lettering," he said as I wrapped my legs around his waist. Maybe this was just an elaborate game of chicken. Maybe he really did want to bang.

"It's a dark wish of somebody else's," I whispered.

He slid his hands under my butt cheeks and pulled me off the stool then, putting me on the floor in front of him. "Stop trying to control the group."

I snorted. As if I was controlling the group.

"Go into the living room and wait for me."

I stood there. Did he really mean to complete the tattoo then and there?

"Is that a Mississippi?" he asked.

I turned and walked into the living room and sat on the tattoo chair in my tank top and yoga pants.

Five minutes later, he was walking in with his box of tattoo gear. He brought over the other chair he always used, setting it next to where I sat, facing away. He had me hang my arm over the back of the chair, which he straddled.

When we were all set up, he began to clean my arm with an

alcohol-soaked cotton ball, all cool and bitey. I tipped my head back, staring at the ceiling. He did the tattoos by stages. We all had the angry lightning clouds on our ankles from before, of course. Now we all had angels on our arms. The angels were beautiful— very gothic with curly scrolls. It seemed like such a shame to inscribe that message.

"This will be so glorious," he said, running his hand over my upper arm. "You must stop trying to control the group," he said again.

"Why?" I looked over, straight into his eyes. "Because that's *your* job? To control the group?"

He looked at me from under dusky lashes. Just that look and I knew I was right. "Are you ready or not?"

"Not that I'm saying I don't want whatever tattoo everybody else gets, but haven't you ever heard of the power of positive thinking? What about that?"

He caressed my arm, admiring his work some more. "How about I take the *fucking-g* power of positive thinking and crush it into a little ball with my vengeance?"

"There you go, that's the spirit."

He got suddenly serious. "This is important to me, Isis."

"A tattoo is forever," I said.

"Precisely," he said softly. "Precisely." There was something about the wistful way he said it that put my intuition on red alert. Something *more* was going on here—what, exactly, I didn't know. Was he still worried about my quitting?

"Of course I'm with you," I said. "But just because I'm dedicated one hundred percent to you doesn't mean I've lost my ability to form my own opinions on things like tattoos."

He whipped out a scarf and tied my arm to the slats of the chair back it hung over.

"What are you doing?"

He stood and walked around to the back of the chair I sat on and tapped the top of my head. "Other arm."

I looked up. What was he up to? He waited. "Fine," I said. I put out my non-tattoo arm and he took it and tied it to the back of the chair. "I already said *yes* on the tattoo. What more do you want?"

He said nothing more, but he wanted something more. What?

He came around to the front of me and straddled my lap, squishing my legs onto the hard, wooden chair. His dark hair brushed his brows. Odin was devilishly handsome, especially when he was being devilish. He toyed with my tank top strap, just a little bit dangerous, a little bit off the rails.

"You don't have to tie me up for a tattoo. How can you even work on my arm like this?"

"Maybe I like you like this, goddess," he said softly, letting his fingers drop to my hardened nipples. "Helpless."

Wellllll...maybe I liked it, too.

He rolled a nipple gently between his fingers, sending ripples of pleasure through me. I watched his beautiful eyes, attempting to maintain my calm even as warmth intensified in my core. I was sure something was up, and I needed to know what it was and not be distracted by sex. What was he not saying about the tattoo?

"High emotions always make you so much more sensitive," he whispered. "As does immobility."

I really was immobile with him heavy on me like that. He flicked the nipple, and it was all I could do to not gasp with pleasure. He said, "I'm going to give you this tattoo of hate and vengeance, and then maybe I'll fuck you."

"Every girl's dream date," I said.

He kissed down my neck to my collarbone.

"My question is, where does it end?" I added.

He fingered the underside of one breast, lifting it and suckling it through the fabric of my tank top, creating an exciting roughness on my nipple. "Where do you think it ends?"

My voice went husky, but I would not be swayed. "Nowhere, that's where. The three of you were screwed by your own people,

I get it. But an agency can't suddenly be horrified at its own mistakes and cry and beg for mercy, right? You can never feel satisfaction of vengeance from an *organization*. It's stupid to try."

He pulled away and traced my lips with his fingers. "Stupid and smart has nothing to do with it. I wish you could hear that. I wish you could be with us in that."

He invaded my mouth with a kiss, just because he could. Letting me know he'd take me how he wanted.

It was a mad turn-on.

"You think anybody is really operating on stupid versus smart?" he asked between kisses. "You think you are?"

"Of course."

"You do?" He kissed me long and strong, tongue like a rough snake.

My breath sped as he smoothed his hands down my neck, down to my breasts. He closed his fingers around my nipples and squeezed, sending bolts of feeling through to my pussy.

I shut my eyes, teetering on the knife-edge of the unknown. "Odin—"

"Look where you are right now," he whispered. "Look at your life—you're a fugitive. You let three outlaws have sex with you whenever they please."

"Your point?"

He trailed his fingers down my belly, down into my yoga pants, and to my drenched panties. He shifted and pushed the fabric aside, touching me with just one finger, sliding it gently in between my folds, amber eyes fixed on mine. I drew up at the feeling of his finger, which he slid back and forth. "Most people would think it's stupid, how you're living."

"I don't care," I gasped as he circled his finger around on my sensitive nub now.

I was utterly under his control, now.

He stroked expertly, toying with me.

I fought the feeling, but I was losing my train of thought a little. There was something I was trying to find out!

He added a finger, lengthening his strokes. "So you would say that it is objectively smart, Isis, to become what you have become?" He pushed two fingers fully inside me now.

"Probably," I gasped as he curled and moved them in a diabolically delicious way. "Oh, God," I said.

He took over the stroking with his thumb and fucked me with his fingers, taking me in a lewd, hot way. "Would all of this seem smart to an outside observer?" he whispered into my ear, and then he pulled his face away and watched my eyes as he continued to pleasure me, blotting out my thoughts with his clever fingers.

It was a little unfair, him carrying on this conversation with me while he was getting me off.

"What do you say, Isis? Do you prefer to operate on stupid and smart, or something else entirely?"

"You're not being fair," I gasped.

"You love a good power imbalance," he whispered.

He loved it, too. He loved when I was melty and helpless. We all did!

And this new twist now, simultaneously asking me hard questions while destroying my train of thought. It was the intellectual version of being bound and helpless and fucked by a fully clothed man.

"Would this seem stupid to an outside observer?"

"I don't care," I gasped, belly lit up with feeling.

"Because you just want it," he added.

"Yes," I gasped. "I just want it."

"You just fucking want it."

"Yes," I repeated.

"Precisely," he whispered. And he finger fucked me in a new way, thumb playing on my sensitive clit, owning me, controlling me.

I tried to focus, knowing I'd just conceded some sort of point, but my entire being was too busy melting under his clever fingers, and finally I broke apart in a thousand-star orgasm, and all I could do was ride it, panting, shattering, as I came.

When I focused my eyes, I saw him standing over me, cock visibly hard in his jeans. "Sometimes you just want what you want, even if it doesn't seem smart. We want vengeance. The Prime."

He went back to the empty chair and used another scarf to bind my wrist even more firmly to the slats.

So all of that had just been to drive a point home?

"That's one technique they never taught us in debate class," I said.

He didn't think that was funny. He kept tying me up. He wanted me all roped up. He still had that hard-on going, and I guessed he was on some sort of jag.

"You and your ski jumps and things," he continued. "Bungie jumping. Do you see us infantilizing you by telling you what you should and shouldn't want?"

He really wanted me to understand, but how could I? It was dangerous. Shouldn't there be a line drawn at danger?

"Come and fuck me," I said. "I know you want to fuck me."

"I need to get these on before the Prime." He continued to bind my wrist.

"Why the hurry? I'm so wet right now. It would feel so good to have you inside me."

The truth.

"Stop it. You're getting your tattoo."

"You don't have to tie me. It's insulting."

"Is that a Mississippi?" He tightened the scarf and then took up the tool, question in his eyes.

"Then do it," I bit out. "If the group is getting the tattoo, I'm getting the tattoo."

"Good." He started up the implement.

"Put it on there," I said, lying back. "You *wish* we were dead, motherfuckers. Just tattoo that dark wish right on me."

"So I will." And he started. I could feel the little needle prick and bite my skin. It hurt, but not as much as the sense that this was some kind of horrible turning point toward darkness and crashing and burning instead of a viable future.

But whatever happened, I was with my guys. I loved them.

"Put the whole goddamn thing on there. I want to die a fiery death with the same tattoo as you guys."

"Okay, goddess."

Needless to say, that wasn't the answer I was fishing for.

I was hoping for something along the lines of *We're not going to die, Isis!*

Chapter Fourteen

I CLOSED MY EYES, FEELING UNCOMFORTABLY IN TOUCH with all the immutable laws of the universe, especially the one where beautiful, brilliant things had to die, like comets burning out from their bright fire.

Odin had given me his *walk away* lecture quite strongly recently—just the other day when we were out sitting on the bank. He'd pointed out a few alleys that would be good to head down if things went bad.

You walk away if you can, he'd instructed.

It was usually a dance when my guys said stuff like that, because I'd always insist that it wouldn't come to a firefight, and they'd be like, *But if it does.* Like when somebody elderly makes statements about dying, and you say that's a long way off, but you both know it really might not be.

I could feel the hole in my heart already, like they were already dead. A sob escaped my throat.

"I'm not hurting you."

A horrible idea seized me. "Why are you so eager to get these tattoos on before the Prime? Why does it have to be before?"

The buzzing stopped. "Pull yourself together."

It was too late. Tears clotted my eyes.

God! How self-centered I was! All this time I was thinking about the tattoos as a power struggle, a failure on Thor and Zeus's and especially Odin's part to understand how negative they were.

I wasn't thinking.

I wasn't listening.

"You don't think you'll survive the Prime," I said. "You don't want to go out with your masterpiece unfinished."

"Do I need a gag for you, too?"

"I'm right, aren't I? You don't think we'll survive."

He was silent for a long time. Then he said, "I think *you* will, goddess."

He started up the tool.

My belly nearly dropped through the floor. "You think you're going to die on this job, and you're still going for it?"

"The Prime is the most glorious prize, and the most upsetting to our enemies. It's reckless, but I can't stop wanting to rob it. You of all people should understand."

I tried to move my arm away from him, but I was immobilized. I was moving enough that he couldn't tattoo it. Again he turned off the tool. "What?"

"Do the others know you think that?"

His eyes went dark. "It doesn't matter. It won't change anything."

"So they don't know? How can you not let them know? Like, hey, I have a bad feeling on this one. Like we might *die*." I could barely believe I was saying the words.

"Talking about it would just make it worse. Don't make me regret being honest with you," Odin said. "I respected you enough to answer your question truthfully."

"They have to know, Odin. You have to tell them."

"It's not how we do things, Isis," he said. "We all have different feelings about jobs, but we go ahead and do them, because it's what we do."

"They can't pull it off if you refuse to go."

"I would never refuse to go. I want to rob it as much as Zeus and Thor do. Anyway, a bad feeling could mean many things."

I regarded him wildly. "I don't want you to die."

He touched my chin. "A bad feeling doesn't mean we'll die."

"But it could. Is this foolish?" I wondered. "I'm going to stop this."

"You can't."

"Odin." I felt the tears prick my eyes.

"Don't try. It's a mountain we must climb. You want us to stop being who we are? To retire in your *fucking-g* brochure?"

My heart beat wildly. "I don't want you to stop being who you are! But why are those the only two choices? Rob the most glittering bank in the world or fish like old men? I want another choice."

"Giving up on the Prime feels like giving up on life," he said. "Do you remember what Zeus said when we first decided to get these tattoos?" Calmly, he inspected his work. "He said that we're a family now and that means we can be as messed up as we want to be. That we will support each other in our messed-up ways and belong together. We're messed up, Ice."

Shivers rained over my skin. My throat felt too clogged to speak.

"We accept you as nobody else ever has," he continued. "Can't you do the same for us? We need to rob the Prime, even if it's foolhardy."

He was right in that they did support me in every one of my desires, my goals, my dreams. Well, short of dressing as tights-wearing woodsmen and brutishly ravishing me in a forest like in the cartoon porn I enjoyed.

But in general, they did.

"Did we force you to return to your sheep farm?" he continued.

"I don't want you to die."

"We can't just *not die*; we have to live, Ice." He started up his tattoo implement as if that were the end of that. "Even if it means dying."

"So...what, then?" I bit out. "Death is your endgame?"

"Death is everybody's endgame."

A tear slid down my cheek.

"Screw you," I sobbed. "I'm telling them that you have a bad feeling."

"It won't change anything."

"Fuck off if I don't want you to die," I gasped, feeling another tear roll down my cheeks.

He stopped the thing again and ran a finger gently over my elbow. "The worst thing about death would be leaving you, goddess."

"Odin," I said, tears rolled openly and wantonly down my cheeks now, and I was gripped with this wild, irrational feeling. "Put it on, then. I want it now. The whole tattoo."

Sounds came from the foyer. The door. "We're back," Zeus called from the other room. Clinks in the kitchen. Putting away bottles.

I started crying even harder now. I loved them so much!

There was a blur of motion from the right.

Big hands grabbed Odin by his shirtfront.

Zeus.

Odin's tattoo tool went flying as Zeus threw him against the wall with a resounding thud. "What the fuck are you doing to her? Why's she crying?"

"I'm giving her the tattoo."

"She's crying! If she doesn't want to have a tattoo, she doesn't have to get one."

"Stop it!" I said. "I want the tattoo! Let him be!"

Thor was at my back, untying me. "God, Odin."

"Stop it! I want the tattoo," I said.

"Then why are you tied up and crying?" Zeus demanded.

"Because I'm worrying about the Prime."

Zeus gave me a serious look. "You know we'll be brilliant, goddess." He let Odin down and stalked over to me. "Let's see."

Thor had just untied my arm and freed it. I held it out so that Zeus could inspect my tattoo, which was all red and puffy like they get. "Motherfuckers," he read. "I think it looks good."

"That's all that it says?"

"So far," Zeus said. "A blank part of a scroll and then *motherfuckers*."

Thor returned with a bottle of champagne and four glasses. "Seriously, Odin? You had to do it now?"

Odin returned to his seat and dabbed my arm. "I want to finish them."

I took a deep breath. "Odin wants to complete the tattoos because he has a bad feeling about the Prime." I could feel Odin's gaze boring into me, but I kept on, looking straight at Zeus and then at Thor. "He has a bad feeling, and I think you guys need to consider canceling it."

"Odin." Zeus frowned. "You worried we'll die?"

"Not specifically, it's just a bad feeling," Odin said.

"For how long?" Thor asked.

"A few days," Odin said.

Zeus's voice was full of emotion. "That's why you want our tattoos complete."

"We can't go out with them partway done," Odin said.

I waited. Surely they would reconsider their dangerous plans now.

"Well, let's get going!" Zeus popped a cork. "That would be fucked up to die like that with an unfinished tattoo message of nothing."

"That's not what's fucked up," I said.

Thor kneeled and inspected. "We'll be getting tattooed all night at this rate, but it's going to look awesome."

"Odin has a bad feeling!" I said.

Thor looked up at me with his blue, blue eyes. "We all get bad feelings now and then, goddess. A bad feeling is never a reason to stop."

"Says who? A million years of human evolution? Oh, wait, a million years of human evolution says just the opposite."

"Actually, a hundred thousand years," Thor said.

"Oh, a hundred thousand years," I said, tears threatening. "Chump change."

"Don't cry, goddess." Zeus put a muscular arm around me.

"We'll be fine," Thor said. "I have a good feeling about the Prime. Shouldn't that balance out Odin's bad feeling?"

I sniffed, shocked they were going through with it. I had to find a way to stop them, but not one that would mess up the robbery or get them arrested. I was just the driver; it wasn't like my refusal to participate would prevent the heist. Because one of the *Gigis* could always drive.

Zeus pushed the hair from my eyes. "Hey. A bad feeling never killed anybody."

Odin brought me a glass of champagne. I took it with a scowl.

Everybody agreed we could all get *motherfuckers* on our arms, and then Odin would put *You WISH we were dead* on it later tonight.

"My turn," Zeus said, sticking out his arm.

"Hold on." Odin bandaged my tattooed area, and then he held onto my arm and looked up at me. "Two hours you leave that," he said.

I nodded.

"Okay, *motherfuckers* for you," Odin said to Zeus. "The rest tomorrow."

He cleaned Zeus's arm and started up his tool.

Thor slid in on the other side of me so that I was sandwiched between him and Zeus.

I downed my drink.

We never drank and stayed out late the night before a job—it was critical to go into a robbery fresh as a daisy, but two days before, that's when the party was. The *penultimate party*, Thor called it. He refilled my glass.

There was still time to stop this thing. Two days.

Matteo arrived with more booze and three pizzas while Odin was working on Thor's arm. He took a look at the work and laughed. "You guys are bonkers."

Aside from Thor, who was effectively on call, we were all pretty bombed at the point where they put the dance music on.

I was finishing my fifth slice of pizza at that point. Zeus and Matteo were dancing.

Odin settled in on the couch. "Come here, Isis."

I walked over there and stood in front of him, looking down. I'd changed into a mod silk hot pants one-piece outfit with strappy sandals for the party, and Odin had seemed to like it most of anybody, though nobody had fucked me yet. It was giving me a complex. I frowned.

"What?" Odin asked innocently.

"You know what," I said.

"Oh, come here." Odin patted his lap. I settled in with the champagne bottle and stretched my legs out on top of his. We had matching arm bandages. He'd done his own tattoo, of course.

"Hey," he said. "Look at me."

I leaned my head back on his shoulder and looked up at him.

He smoothed my hair back and then grabbed it in one hand and pulled my head to make me meet his eyes, like I wasn't already doing that. "Don't try to stop the robbery."

"I don't like that you have that bad feeling."

I could feel his cock harden under my ass, and his gaze changed in the way it sometimes did when he was thinking sex. My heart beat like mad. And then he kissed me. I melted a little bit inside. "Don't try to stop it," he whispered, "or you'll jinx it."

"There's no such thing as jinxing."

"Not true. A robbery is a psychophysical play of circumstances, don't you agree, Thor?"

Thor settled down on the other end of the couch. He turned sideways and put his feet up on my lap. "I would agree."

Odin turned my head and kissed me more insistently than he usually did. His cock seemed to almost harden under my ass. "You like an audience, Ice," he whispered. "Do you want Thor and me to fuck you in front of Matteo?"

I looked up at Matteo, robot dancing a few feet away from us. "He's *robot dancing*," I said.

Thor snickered.

I cast a sly glance at Odin. "Are you trying to distract me and cloud my mind again with your new debate method?"

"Always." Odin kissed me again.

It was then that the Gigis arrived, though arrived might be an understatement. More like busted in, picking the lock, setting off the alarm. Macy wore silver pants and a bright blue halter top, and she went right at Matteo. Angel and Jenny were there, too. Angel had a gun.

"Hey, bitches, no shooting in the house," Zeus said as Macy shoved Matteo backwards into a plant.

"What the fuck?" Matteo said.

"You're doing the Prime Royale? That's our fucking bank," said Angel.

"Who says we're doing the Prime?" Matteo protested

"You were sitting out there all day. We heard about it," Jenny said. "You think we're idiots?"

"You don't do banks," Thor said. "You guys are residential."

"We were going to make an exception," Angel said. "It was Macy's idea how to get the codes."

We all looked at Matteo. Odin wasn't happy, but I was overjoyed. Would the Gigis wreck everything? Odin still had my hair. He pulled, just to remind me. "Don't get your hopes up, goddess," he whispered. "We'll let them help if worse comes to worse."

Macy and Matteo were yelling at each other, with the other Gigis chiming in; I was starting to feel embarrassed, like maybe they needed to hash it out somewhere else.

Odin gave me a nudge in the direction of the porch. "Go clean yourself up," he said.

"Excuse me?"

"Go." He lowered his voice to be extra gravelly. "Clean yourself up in the porch shower."

That was the shower we usually used before getting in the hot tub. "I'm not supposed to soak with the tattoo for two weeks, I thought," I said.

"Nobody's going in the hot tub," he growled.

My entire core tightened. *Clean yourself up* sometimes preceded very dirty plans.

Thor stood. "I need to check in south of the border." I was guessing he didn't mean that sexily. He headed out to the bedroom. Zeus had gone into the kitchen. Everybody wanted to leave Matteo and the Gigis alone.

"Way to break up a party," I grumbled at the Gigis, not that they could hear me. I actually really liked them.

I headed out to the porch, walking in my bare feet across the shadowed porch timbers, which were still warm from the day of sun. I went into the little cedar shower stall and turned on the water, apprehensive and sort of excited, too, like I often was when they made me do pre-sex things. It stoked the anticipation.

I stripped off my clothes and began dousing myself, waiting for Odin and whoever else to join me.

I heard a swish in the trees. I assumed it was squirrels, maybe, up there playing, though it registered as slightly odd. I turned around and let the water beat down on my face.

I sensed movement behind me. Odin? Zeus?

Suddenly, a rough, gloved hand clapped over my mouth and an arm went around my torso like a steel trap.

Alarm shot through me. The arm wore an unfamiliar shirt, and worse, smelled unfamiliar. Like chemical-scented body spray.

My guys never wore body spray!

The next thing I knew, I was breathing in something sickly sweet from a cloth over my mouth.

I kicked and fought, praying for Odin to come out and surprise the guy—I was sure it was the feather guy.

It was suddenly delicious to sleep, and my last thought was that squirrels don't play in trees at night, and I should've known that.

Chapter Fifteen

I WOKE UP ON AN UNCOMFORTABLE PATCH OF STICKS and dirt.

What?

I was in some sort of forest.

I rose up, stabilizing myself against a nearby tree trunk, eyes straining to see in the faint moonlight, ears alert for any sound beyond the crickets and the rustle of breeze high up in the treetops.

Memories started falling into place. The shower. The rough hand. The smell, so *not* my guys. I'd been drugged and brought here.

The horrible thought came to me that I could've been raped while I was unconscious, but in the next moment, I knew that I hadn't.

Still, my heart pounded in my chest. Everything seemed surreal. Even the slim crescent moon in the sky. I could hear highway sounds, but it was hard to pinpoint the direction they were coming from.

I wrapped my arms around myself, feeling woozy, breathing deeply, trying to clear the cobwebs from my brain.

Determine where you are, I told myself.

No city lights were visible to orient me. If I ran the wrong way, I'd be going deeper into wilderness. I gazed up at the moon, sitting senselessly on the side of the sky. Unlike the sun, which rises in the east and sets in the west, the fucking moon just flits all around.

Thanks, moon, I thought. *Thanks a lot!*

I tried to listen, smell, straining to figure out if I was maybe near the ocean. Could I be in the Santa Monica Mountains?

I swallowed, afraid to make a move, like I might alert my captor, who surely was out there, watching. Was this some part of a sick game? I'd seen a few movies where people were dropped in the wilderness as human prey. Could that be what was going on?

With a sick feeling, I remembered the feather guy. But he was in the hospital, right?

I sucked in more huge breaths, trying to wake myself up, thinking I should focus on finding a weapon.

It was then I noticed my clothes. I'd been dressed in some sort of a skimpy, tattered little dress, like a figure skater might wear if she were playing an impoverished waif or something. Maybe skating to the theme song of *Les Miserables* or *Peter Pan*. The skirt had jagged panels of fabric, and I had no panties on. And pointy cloth moccasins.

Well, there was one clue about who had done this. It was somebody who hated good fashion!

And then I took another look at the outfit. Because it looked strangely familiar. I realized then that it was what the elf girl in the forest wears in the woodsman cartoon porn.

Was it my guys behind this? I couldn't be sure. I kept coming back to the smell of my abductor.

The smell had been all wrong. And the way he touched me. And drugged me. Did my abductor know my cartoon porn habit?

Somewhere in the distance behind me, a stick snapped. Then there was a crunch. A footstep.

Adrenaline shot through me, and on instinct, I took off running—no easy thing in the thin moccasins.

More footsteps sounded behind me—*crunch, crunch, crunch.* The footsteps increased, both in volume and number. Suddenly a dark, hooded figure stepped into my path.

I screamed and turned, heading back the other way, only to run smack into the very solid chest of another hooded man.

"Zeus?" I said. He felt like Zeus.

Hands grabbed me from behind and a sack was thrown over my head. It was scratchy, like burlap.

"You guys?" I cried out. "Come on," I pleaded.

Surely it was them, cleverly fooling me.

"You have to tell me if it's you or else it's not fun!"

I was carried a ways and laid onto a strange, rough wooden platform. I tried to wriggle and kick away. A third man had joined the first two, or at least it seemed like a third one was there. He was trying to lock my kicking feet into cuffs.

"Come on," I said. "I know it's you." Or, I was pretty sure.

A pair of hands stood me upright on the wooden platform; another pair of hands locked each of my ankles into a wide stance, via a spreader bar, it seemed.

No way could I run with that thing on. I flailed wildly; at one point, my knee connected. Somebody grunted, gripping my ankle harder and forcing it into place, until I was locked onto this strange platform.

"Odin?"

More hands lifted my hands up so that they were level with my ears. Something smooth and wooden grazed the front of my neck and the front of my wrists, like my neck and my wrists were being eased into semi-circles that had been cut into wood.

"I know it's you," I said hopefully through the hot burlap.

Something grazed the back of my neck and the backs of my wrists. And then there was a click.

It was as if two sets of semi-circles had fitted together, trapping my neck in a large circle and my wrists in smaller circles. This board thing forced me to stand upright in a kind of goalpost position, spread-legged. My chin rested on the smooth, wooden edge of the hole.

The elf-girl in the forest was often put in configurations like this by the evil woodsmen.

I yanked and squirmed to no avail. I moved my hands around; something else clicked and my palms came into contact with two knobs I could grip onto. My hands closed instinctively around them.

All I heard was the rustling of leaves. I stood there, trembling, blinded by the bag on my head. I used the knobs to pull up my weight and kick out my feet, spreader bar and all. I came into contact with nothing but air.

Large, rough hands caressed my hips, and I jerked. They went away and then came back again. There was something familiar about the touch.

"Oh my God," I breathed, still woozy.

A voice. "Shh."

The bag was whisked off my head—finally—and I gulped in the cool air. A large, hooded figure stood in front of me, shrouded in shadows aside from where the moonlight hit one of his big, black boots, which was scuffed up in a rather familiar way...

"Jesus!" I said. "Zeus!"

No answer. A hand brushed my hair from my eyes.

"You guys?"

"Shh."

"Come on, say something!"

The figure before me stepped closer, into a shaft of moonlight; I could see now that he wore a green hat, green tunic, green tights, and boots. I'd recognize his big body anywhere. *Zeus.*

"Oh my God!" I said, slightly pissed off. "Zeus! You scared me!"

"I don't know who Zeus is, elf," Zeus growled from under the hood.

I jerked my arms downward, trying to free myself. "Let me out of this."

A hand slid around and touched my breast through the little dress. "This can go easy or this can go hard, elf-girl." *Thor.*

"You scared me!" I said, heart pounding. I didn't know whether to be angry or what. They were reenacting my favorite cartoon porn storyline. But seriously, they'd gone pretty far, abducting me like that. Though, to be fair, it's similar to what happens in the cartoon. Except she was gathering flowers in the forest at the time. And they don't drug her.

Odin, also in a hood and tights, came up beside me and grabbed my hair. If I hadn't known it was him, I'd have certainly known by the way he grabbed my hair. "We can ravish you easy or hard," he said. "Your choice."

"What?" I asked stupidly.

"It's a real question, elf."

My heart pounded in my chest. My bank robbers wearing *tights*. For me. "You're all in tights," I said.

It was sweet. I was into costumes, but they typically weren't. And here they were in tights! And they'd created this platform, which had clearly been modeled on one of my favorite dirty cartoon porn scenarios. Had they built it themselves?

The more I thought about it, the more I hoped so. Because how exactly would they have explained the device to whatever carpenter they'd hired?

Zeus disappeared from my view.

"Easy or hard, answer the question," Odin said from under his hood. I couldn't see their faces. It was wild and hot, and I found myself trembling with a mixture of leftover fear, but also excitement.

"You think I'm putty in your hands now? You think I'll just do what you want?"

By way of answer, Odin's hand tightened in my hair. The woodsmen ravished her hard in the scenarios I favored.

"I won't answer your stupid questions," I said.

I could feel Zeus watching me from under his hood, and I heard Thor rustling around back there. I felt my nipples tighten under the wimpy fabric.

"Hard, then," Odin said.

I gripped the smooth knobs. My blood raced.

A finger lifted my skirt from behind and tucked it up into the bodice of my outfit. I could feel the cool night breeze on my bare ass. One finger trailed down my tender ass skin, tracing a lazy design of some sort. It was like my entire soul focused on that finger, what it would do next, where it would travel.

A delicious warmth spread through my nether regions as I yearned for the finger to travel further southward and inward.

Odin let go of my hair.

It was here I realized I was panting.

Crunching footsteps sounded as Zeus approached. Even when he was near, I couldn't see his face from under the hood. They'd positioned me so that the moon would be behind them when they stood in front of me. Unlike me, my hunky bank robbers knew exactly where the moon would be when.

Zeus said, "We're going to have some fun with you unless you tell us to stop, and I think you know what that means."

Mississippi, he meant.

He touched something to my belly through the fabric. Because of the way my head was trapped, I couldn't tip my head to look down and see what it was, which made it all the more exciting in a scary way.

I thought it might be a stick until he brought it up near my face and touched my cheek with it.

A riding crop.

My eyes widened.

"Do you? Do you know what it means?" he persisted.

They'd never used one of those before. "Yes," I gasped.

"Good." He walked back to where he'd originally stood and set the crop against a tree. Then he lifted his tunic, just enough for me to see his huge package barely contained within the stretchy green fabric. It was all wrong in a way that turned me on.

"Get the elf ready for me," he said. An actual line from one of the cartoons.

"Oh my God," I panted as one of my guys pressed against me from behind, sending waves of feeling through me.

A hand snaked around my hip.

Fingers parted my hot folds, delving in, caressing my clit.

I closed my eyes, melting with desire.

The finger moved and stroked through the hot slickness between my legs—slowly. Excruciatingly slowly.

I tried to move against it, to create some pressure, but my guys could be a little evil.

My legs strained to come together, but the spreader bar prevented it.

Thor—it had to be him—was driving me a little wild.

Another hand reached around and brushed my nipple.

"She's ready," Thor said.

Zeus reached up as if he might be about to remove his hood.

"Stop! Keep the hood on," I gasped.

Zeus stilled his hands. Grunted.

"You think pretty elves walking around in forests get a say in that kind of thing?" Odin asked.

"No," I breathed as rough hands parted my butt cheeks. And the hood stayed on.

"Important that you know that, elf," Odin said.

I gasped as his finger gently spread lube over the pucker of my asshole. I closed my eyes, feeling everything acutely, as though my asshole had grown extra nerve endings, and whoever it was back there was exploring each and every one of them, roaming over all the little folds and the tiniest creases. I imagined him pressing inward. I craved that he would, but he just kept circling, teasing.

I opened my eyes to come face to face with Zeus's dark hood. It sent a zing of heat into my belly.

The finger pushed in just a tiny bit behind me, then out.

In the cartoon, the elf girl begs and cries for them to stop while they touch her and fuck her. I didn't want Thor to stop, but I wondered what it would be like, to fully playact it.

A part of me wanted to fully playact it. The begging. The distress. But if I cried, they might stop.

Zeus cast aside the crop and brought his hands to his crotch, and the next thing I knew, he was ripping a hole in the tights. With sure, strong movements, he freed his cock, huge and thick and pale, jutting out from the smooth green fabric. "Strip her," he commanded.

Rough hands behind me ripped off my waifish little dress, destroying it, no doubt. It was in the zone I couldn't see.

The fabric fell away, and I was naked, trapped there. And the hoods seemed even more psycho now in a way that majorly turned me on.

Zeus came to me then, head on. Hands behind me grabbed underneath my ass, supporting me as Zeus lifted my spread legs up so that his jutting exposed cock was positioned right against my hot, wet sex.

"Oh," I said. He was Zeus, but also this hooded woodsman, about to plunder the elf girl.

"Feel it," Odin whispered into my ear as Zeus pressed the fat tip of his cock partly into me, easing it in by increments.

I breathed, feeling it.

"You're not struggling enough," Odin added. "It seems to me that elves who are ravished in forests should be a little more upset."

"What?" I asked.

"It seems to me," Odin said, speaking slowly this time, "that if you don't seem distressed enough, we'll distress you."

In the perfect choreography that was my bank robbers, the finger at my ass was gone, replaced by a hard slap.

"Ow!" I cried, more from the surprise.

"Beg us to stop," Odin said, grabbing my hair.

Zeus withdrew, still hanging onto my thighs. His cock bobbed against my sex.

I looked into Odin's faceless hood. In a low voice, he said, "Act distressed like the elf in the cartoon, or I'll whip you until you really are distressed. She's distressed when the fucking starts."

How many times had they watched that thing?

"Maybe she doesn't want to be that elf girl," Zeus said.

"Do you want to be that elf girl?" Odin asked.

"Yes, let me be her," I gasped. "I want to be like her."

"Then be like her," Zeus growled, getting with the program now.

Just then something large, hard, and cool pressed into my asshole.

It was so much feeling—too much goodness.

"Don't, please," I whimpered.

Zeus pulled my thighs wider as Thor kept forcing the thing in, penetrating me, invading me. "Please, no," I gasped, even though I meant the opposite.

With one hand, Zeus set the smooth, hot tip of his cock into me; with a massive thrust, he pushed in, filling me.

I cried out.

"*Be like her*," he growled as he started banging into me, hands gripping the backs of my thighs, supporting my weight and holding my knees apart. My ankles were still separated with the spreader bar, which he hit with his knees with every thrust, forcing my ankles back, over and over.

"Stop!" I cried. "It hurts!"

My cries made him thrust all the harder. I couldn't believe the thrilling intensity of it, saying no and begging, and him still fucking me.

Odin said, "Any elf we find in the forest, we get to do whatever we *fucking-g* want to you."

"No," I cried. "Please!"

Still, Zeus fucked me. It was as if I'd entered the elf girl's world of magic and forbidden urges.

Thor had shoved the smooth thing all the way into my asshole now. He simply left it there, which made the fucking extra intense.

"Cry," Odin growled.

His command sparkled darkly through my core, and I whimpered and cried best I could, but it felt fake.

My belly went lopsided as Odin strolled over to the tree to take up the riding crop.

"Take the bar off her feet, Thor," he said.

"No!" I cried, kind of meaning it. Because, why the bar off now? What did he have in mind? The woodsmen did all sorts of fucked up things to the elf girl.

Zeus stopped thrusting and stilled inside me as unseen hands worked at my ankles, undoing the cuffs.

"Don't hurt me," I panted as a fully hooded Odin walked around and came up behind me, touching the end of the riding crop to my cheek, caressing me gently. "Do you want the bag over your head again?"

"No," I said.

The bar fell with a clank. My ankles felt lighter.

He took the crop from my cheek and disappeared behind me.

Trees rustled above, and I became acutely aware of the breeze on my naked ass and Zeus's fingers curling into the underside of my thighs. He was still hard inside me, but he didn't move. I waited, heart pounding.

A whistle. A whap. A sting. "Ow!" I jerked in surprise at the bite of pain on my ass cheek, shocked at how much it hurt.

I squeezed my pussy around Zeus's hard cock. He groaned and tightened his grip on my thighs.

Odin said, "If you don't cry like an elf girl should, you'll get the bag back over your head."

I whimpered. I didn't want that—seeing them hooded was part of the dream.

"Thor is going to pull that thing out of your ass now and shove his giant cock in there no matter how much you beg him not to," Odin said. "And then Zeus is going to fuck you. Do you think both of their giant cocks will fit in your tiny elf holes?"

"No," I breathed.

Odin put his face to my cheek and grabbed my hair again—hard. "They'll make them fit." He let go and disappeared once more. Thor took the thing out of my ass. I felt the cool air again. I gripped tighter to the knobby things above my wrist holes, bracing myself.

Another whistle sounded through the air, followed by a sharp crack. Pain exploded over my ass—one, two, three cruel whips of the crop.

"Ow!" I screamed, a little angry at the intensity. "God, you don't have to—"

"Shut up, elf!" Odin hit me twice more—weirdly hard stings.

I began to cry for real now. It was as if the unexpected pain opened up a floodgate to my emotions, my libido.

Zeus pulled his cock out of me, but he kept hold of my legs, keeping them bent open for Thor, behind me.

"When we saw you in the forest like that, we had to capture you," Odin said. "To use you exactly like this."

Thor positioned his cock at the entrance to my asshole.

"Not that! Let me go!" I sobbed.

Odin stroked my hair softly. "Sorry, elf girl. This is how the woodsmen must take their pleasure from you."

I wept ecstatically as Thor's hard head pushed into my asshole, filling me. He felt so huge going in. So huge.

We'd done this before, but the elf thing made me like a virgin.

"Breathe, elf," Odin whispered. "Let the woodsmen take their pleasure."

I cried out as Thor thrust into my ass.

"You like that?" Odin asked.

"It's too big!"

"Relax and it'll be over, elf girl." Odin said. Odin slid the tip of the crop along the underside of my breast—a threat that prompted more warm tears to stream down my cheeks. I felt crazily primal.

Thor started fucking me in the ass, wild and harsh and primitive.

"Please!"

"We'll do whatever we want to you," Odin said, caressing my breast with his finger now.

"I can't...I can't..." I panted, not bothering to make sense. It was as though we were four beasts, operating from our darkest and most magical beast brains.

"Too bad," Zeus said, pushing inside me now once more, so that they were both fucking me at the same time while supporting my weight.

I shut my eyes tight. "No!" I begged, excited beyond belief.

They fucked me anyway, mercilessly, stoking my pleasure higher.

"Take it," Odin said, warm in my ear, gently rolling my nipple.

The guys fucked me in unison, forcing waves of color into my mind's eye.

"*Uh-uh-uh,*" Zeus said.

Everything felt so beautiful and dangerous. I didn't know if I could contain the intensity.

The feeling inside me began to swell and build, and I knew I was tipping over toward a shattering orgasm. I fought it, wanting the feeling to last, but they wouldn't stop fucking me, wouldn't stop filling me, wouldn't stop building the feeling higher.

I wept—from joy, from pain, from erotic overload. I was the

elf girl, fucked and ravished against her will. Living my full-color dream.

"Stop fighting," Odin said, expertly fingering my nipple with his fingers. "It's no use to fight us." He squeezed it gently.

I exploded into a starry universe of pleasure.

My orgasm rolled through me in wave after wave, pushing me higher and higher, further and further into oblivion, and still they fucked me.

I was boneless with pleasure and still they fucked me.

Zeus cursed as he came, fingers digging into my butt cheeks. Thor cried out, quivering deep inside me.

I don't know how long it was before they let me off that thing.

Rough hands took me down and set me on ground.

Forest debris poked into my bare back as I stared up at the moon, lost in the dream of the elf girl.

Suddenly the moon was blotted out by Odin standing over me, still in his hood, hand on his cock, which he'd pulled out of his tights.

"You think we're done with you now?"

My belly tightened. At the end, one of the woodsmen always jizzed on the elf girl, debasing her hotly.

"Haven't you used me enough, woodsman?".

"Stay still. Stay right there."

Let's just say wild horses couldn't have dragged me away at this point.

He jerked his hand up his cock, once, and then again, and a thick stream of cum landed on my neck, my breasts.

Just like with the elf girl. I sighed happily.

He knelt down next to me. "That's what you get, elf."

I stared up at him, a little bit dazed. "Thank you."

He smiled his dark, devilish smile. "Always," he said. "Anything."

They'd given me this thing I'd wanted without judgment, and they'd even worn tights. Who else in the universe could've given me this, and with such love behind it? I was always saying I loved them, but did I really, if I was trying to change them?

"I'll support you," I whispered. "Whatever you want. Whatever is inside you. I won't fuck with your beautiful mojo. I won't try to stop the robbery."

Zeus knelt down. "What's that?"

Thor kneeled down on the other side of me and wiped the jizz off my neck and breasts with a soft, damp cloth.

"Robbing the Prime in a blaze of glory, I mean," I whispered. "Do it. It will show those who betrayed you that no target is out of your reach. They'll really wish you were dead."

"You're good with it?" Odin asked.

"Yes," I said.

"It'll feel fucking awesome," Thor said. "To clean out the Prime."

"It will be glorious," Odin said.

"And I want the whole tattoo, too," I said. "I'm not just saying it now—it's ours and I want it. That tattoo is us."

"I want it, too," Zeus said. "Is there time now?"

Odin twisted his lips. "I don't think so. I don't want to rush it."

"We'll get it after," Zeus said.

"What do you mean?" And in the next instant, I got it. "Oh," I said. It was nearly dawn. The elf girl thing had taken hours. The robbery was officially tomorrow now. There was tons of prep. Zeus had to go to work and input the code, a dangerous part of the caper. They'd sacrificed completing the tattoos in order to do my elf girl thing.

I swung my gaze to Odin.

"It was worth it," he said. "You'll get it after the robbery, elf-girl," he said.

And at that moment, I loved my bank robbers so hard, I thought my heart might burst.

Chapter Sixteen

MATTEO AND THE GIGIS WERE GONE BY THE TIME WE returned from our wild woodland adventure, but Matteo told us all about it later that day, a Thursday. He'd spilled to Macy about his plan to give her his part of the jewels, that the whole thing was a scheme to win her back. And he reflected responsibility to her, as Odin had suggested.

Macy still didn't believe him.

"Did *you* believe what you said?" Odin asked. "Or are you just saying shit to her?"

Matteo's noncommittal answer showed he didn't quite believe it.

At eleven in the morning, Matteo, Odin, and I sat on the bank. Thor was already inside as a patron.

This was the point where Zeus needed to break away from his crew and go out on the floor and input the security virus in preparation for the robbery tomorrow.

We watched the manager walk down the sunny sidewalk toward the bagel shop. Things would be soft inside. It was time.

"He's out," Odin whispered over the two-way. "I'm killing fuse twenty-three now." This would give Zeus the excuse he needed to be fucking with the panels. He'd be confused and get to the wrong panel first.

"Roger," Zeus whispered back.

I got out and strolled up to the entrance. The doorman opened the door for me. I passed the security guard and then, as if recalling something, I went back and asked him if he had any experience with the high-end mechanic two blocks down. We knew that the guard took the bank fleet there, and that he and the owner had become friendly.

He talked up the mechanic like we knew he would.

Thor sat at the desk across from a low-level banker, looking all Hollywoody in a beautiful red silk shirt, sunglasses perched on his head, asking about checking services.

Through careful logistical manipulation, a sheer, nipple-displaying shirt, and, if you ask me, a bit of leftover elf magic, I'd gotten the guard facing outside as he talked up his friend's business. I was careful not to look over his shoulder at the flurry of activity across the lobby. That would be Zeus, the bumbling subcontractor at the wrong panel. I smiled brightly and listened, pulse racing.

Soon the buzz returned to normal.

I continued in to make my deposit. When I got back out to the Navigator, Odin was grinning. The code was in. Zeus was back on the job.

A bit later, Thor came back out.

We watched the bank until after business hours, satisfied things were normal. Matteo went off to try to iron things out with Macy, and my guys and I went home and engaged in wholesome activities—grilling veggies, drinking healthy juices, and cleaning guns.

We sat on the porch together after dinner, lounging around, discussing the job. Everything was done, everything ahead of schedule—it was kind of amazing.

My eyes fell to Zeus's massive upper arm. Each of us now had just the cherubic angel holding the scroll that said *motherfuckers* on it. The tattoo looked fucking awesome on him, but it wasn't done.

"Odin," I said. "How long to complete that lettering?"

Thor looked up from his book. "We *are* ahead of schedule here."

"An hour or two each," Odin said.

"Let's do it," Zeus said. "Can you?"

Odin looked over at me. "I could."

"Do me first," I said. "We go into this job with everything right."

Odin's eyes glittered. "Get the chair."

Four hours later we were all freshly inked with the full message: *You WISH we were dead, motherfuckers.* I felt happy and free, like even more of a real outlaw than before.

Zeus declared that finishing them had strengthened the psychophysical play of the robbery—like a sign to the universe that the bank robbers were unstoppable. They were so voodoo about robberies, my guys.

Friday morning, my guys and Matteo and I met up bright and early to wipe bullets and study traffic cams. The job wouldn't actually take place until after the close of the business day. The plan was to sit there in shifts all through the day in different vehicles.

We grabbed donuts on the way to the bank block, then found our favorite parking spot and began the long stakeout—minus Zeus, who was, of course, inside with the HVAC crew. Things looked normal. Like many businesses, the Prime was the most lax on Fridays.

"I hope you won't be expecting us to wear tights from now on," Thor said when Matteo was off for a pee break. We hadn't spoken much about the elf and woodsmen role play. Really, what was there to say?

"I hope *you* don't drug and abduct me every time you want to fuck," I said, adjusting a curl on my wig.

Thor snorted. "I wouldn't recommend it simply from a medical standpoint."

"I legit thought you guys were the feather guy," I said. "It freaked me out."

"The feather guy is in jail," Thor said, eyeing the guard out on a smoke break.

"Well, if he had a partner."

"There could never be more than one feather guy," Odin said. "He works alone. It's his profile."

"Though he never did confess," I said.

A strange hush fell down around us. "I know," Odin said finally. Which was way too long to respond to something so obvious.

"What?" I asked.

"Nothing. You know. Who doesn't prefer a confession?" Odin said, eying me. "It's a closure thing."

I lay my head on Thor's shoulder. "I trust you guys." I flicked my gaze to Odin. I'd decided to trust. To trust in everything. I hated that Odin had that bad feeling, but that's something I had to live with. I had thrown in with them all the way. I didn't tell them I hadn't slept at all the night before.

Thor put his arm around me and kissed my hair. "We got you," he whispered.

I smiled. "Woe betide anyone who messes with the God Pack."

Odin laughed, but it was just a courtesy laugh.

He was barely listening.

We all got a little remote before a big job—pulling into ourselves, or sometimes out of ourselves. You had to go somewhere before a heist, that was the thing I'd realized over the months with my robbers. You had to prepare your soul for the intensity.

But this seemed like more. "Something up?" I asked him.

"I'm thinking we could put Thor out here with you."

"What?" Thor protested. "During the job? I'm bag man."

"We're in there for so long," he said. "Leaving Ice unprotected."

Thor said, "Ice can protect herself."

"Yeah, you know you can trust me out here," I protested, feeling a little hurt. "I can handle it. You know I'm on board one hundred percent—"

"It's not that," Odin said. "It's simply...we've got Matteo inside, so why not be safe? There's the fact that Sleazy Travis didn't confess, and I can't stop thinking about that feather," he admitted. "So dirty and dusty. And the pig's blood..."

"Wait, are you worried it isn't him?" I asked. "That it isn't Travis? Like the feather guy is still out there? Because if he's still out there—" *We shouldn't do the Prime,* I was thinking.

Odin touched my hair. "It's this bad feeling, that's all," he said. "I'm looking for every hole and patching it."

"If he's still out there," I said, "it means he's way smarter than we ever could've imagined." I looked back and forth between him and Thor. "He'd know everything about us. He'd be a threat in every way—to all of us."

"So we put Thor out here. Both of you alert and armed. Anyway, I'm quite sure it's Travis."

"But not certain," I said.

"Nothing's ever certain," Thor said. "If feather guy's out there, let him come at us. I'd like to see it. I'll make him sorry."

Matteo was back. Odin floated the idea of Thor staying out. Matteo liked the idea. "We're lighter inside that way, but it's extra muscle outside if we need an assist."

Yeah, he'd never fully trusted me alone on the outside.

The three of them felt it was a good way to adjust the team. I wasn't so sure.

I wondered if the call of it was getting too strong. The riches of it. The beautiful vengeance.

Odin met Zeus in the park over lunch and cleared the new

configuration with him. They had to re-jigger the plans. In one way, it was harder, but they were used to going in with three guys.

Matteo, Thor, Odin, and I waited in the Navigator.

Five o'clock. Almost go time. Zeus was inside the bank, of course, working on the HVAC repairs like a good technician...a good technician about to go bad.

With a deep breath, I climbed out of the car and went to the nearby Starbucks where I purchased a coffee and did a preemptive pee. I'd be stuck in that SUV for at least three hours, likely more, and there'd be no leaving. Thor, being a guy, could rely on Snapple bottles.

For this phase, I wore my long blonde wig as well as a Christian Dior gown, as if I were on my way to some party. If the shit hit the fan, nobody would expect a woman dressed like that to have firearms strapped to her legs.

We watched the HVAC crew leave—in a hurry. Their hurried exit meant that the "emergency call" Odin had arranged for them to receive had worked.

It meant Zeus had been left behind to secure things with one other guy.

Over the next half hour, the bank employees drifted out, too.

The call came. Thor grabbed it. After a terse exchange, he clicked off.

"Go time."

It meant that Zeus had done his part of the job—he'd forced the man left behind with him to leave a message with his family telling them he was hitting a bar after work. The guy would be out cold now, and unlike when I was out cold, he wouldn't be waking up with hunky woodland guys in tights chasing him.

Probably for the best.

Matteo and Odin had keys to the building next door. They were going to zipline across. The only sightline to the angle of entry was from the east, and at 5:45 precisely, the blinding sun would obscure them via window glare.

"Wait." I kissed Odin like I'd kissed Zeus this morning—with all the passion I had. "Set that fucker on fire," I said.

"You be safe, goddess," he said.

"Always," I said, trying not to cry. "You, too."

"Always," he whispered.

I let him go, feeling like my heart might break. I wanted, suddenly, to tell him how much I loved him, to tell them all. But we never talked like that, and it seemed a bad time to start. I wouldn't jinx the job with teary '*I love you*' proclamations.

I shook hands with Matteo, who grumbled jokingly about not getting a kiss.

And just like that, they were gone.

I settled back with Thor, who turned on the radio on low. The plan was for Odin and Matteo to get onto the roof of the bank. Zeus would let them into the mechanical ceiling area. At that point, Odin would go to work dismantling one of the four security systems in operation, activating the virus Zeus had planted yesterday.

We had the stolen codes—another level of security, thanks to that guard with a gambling problem that Matteo and the Gigis knew.

It would take another hour or two to get into the safety deposit boxes where the really expensive jewels were kept.

We were to move the SUV every hour to different pre-planned spots. When they were ready to run, they'd call, and we were to drive to the back of the building next to the bank—that's where they'd come out if everything went smoothly. If things didn't go smoothly, there were plans B, C, and D.

About twenty minutes after they left, Thor got a ping on his phone. He pulled it out and looked at the screen.

"Shit," he said.

"What?"

"Lupe's in labor."

I straightened up. "She's not due for..."

"I know."

"Oh, my God," I said. "Is she okay?"

"For now. Contractions are still far apart. It could be hours. A day." His thumbs flew over the keypad. They used some sort of free IM app to communicate, and I waited as the messages bounced back and forth. He swore.

"You need to be there?"

He flicked his eyes to the Prime. "Sort of."

"Go. It was always going to be just me," I said.

"What about feather guy?"

"I'm on a public street, armed like Rambo in a locked and bulletproof SUV," I said with a bravery I didn't entirely feel. "Let him try me. Anyway, look, Travis had all that evidence in his garbage. He ran. A bad feeling never killed anyone," I said, echoing Odin.

Thor looked down at his phone.

"She's our fugitive sister. Take the Camaro." We had cars stashed around the area. "It's Friday rush hour. You don't have time to waste."

"I don't know."

"It was always going to be just me out here," I repeated. "This is how we trained it."

"Stay alert."

"No, I'm going to take a nap," I joked.

His smile didn't quite reach his eyes. "You sure?"

"Our beautiful sister in crime is having a baby," I said. "I'll stay here and make our enemies wish we were dead for both of us."

He took off. I tried to tell myself it was good luck that he went. Doing something positive would result in a positive robbery outcome.

Five minutes later, A/V Robert Manning was knocking on the passenger window.

Chapter Seventeen

I stared in confusion as Manning knocked on the window again and again. What the hell was he doing?

I didn't want to unlock the door and let him in, but I couldn't have him out there drawing attention to me—I still had forty-five minutes to go in this position.

I cracked the window. "What's going on?"

"Hello, miss. I just noticed it was you." He smiled the smile of a man confident of his charms. In some universe, maybe. "How's it going?" he asked.

"I can't talk," I said, all terse and businesslike.

He didn't leave.

My heart pounded. How was he not getting it?

He was in the scene. Not only in the scene, but he was a highly trained military man and security guy.

A cop car crawled down the street, slowly.

"Catch you later," I said, a pretty direct message. "Okay?"

He launched into something about the hookup for the front door camera and a rain shield, whatever that was. He wanted to swing by and check out this rain shield. He thought it could short out the whatever thingy, though to give him his due, he used more technical sounding words than that.

It wasn't his words that sent the cold, cold feeling spreading through me.

It was me suddenly knowing it was him. I knew it deep in my bones.

Manning was the feather guy.

He seemed to recognize right when I got it. I tried to put up the window, but he shoved a gun muzzle in there.

Shit!

A scratching at the door. He was picking the lock.

I could practically feel the blood drain from my cheeks.

With shaking hands, I grabbed the keys, fit them into the ignition, and started the engine. He wouldn't shoot me—not out here. Before I could throw it into drive, he was sliding into the passenger seat, gun on me, end fat with a silencer.

I grabbed the phone, thinking to give the abort code.

"Don't you dare, bitch." In a flash, Manning had the phone. But it gave me the opportunity to grab the barrel of his gun. Quickly I got both hands involved, twisting it so that it pointed out the windshield. My arms and hands strained, trying to get the gun. He started forcing it around slowly. I put all my might into not letting him, but he was too strong, too big. I let go when he pointed it back at me.

"That was stupid. You want me to pull the trigger?" he asked, close to me now, breath stinky and warm.

"You'd get arrested."

"Oh, I don't know. They might be a lot more interested in what's happening inside the Prime. If I were to tell them. Who knows? Maybe I'll say I'm here stopping you."

My blood went cold.

"I'll say you're part of the gang," I said. "And that I'm here to stop *you.*"

"Is that your story? Because I'm willing to take that chance. I think they'll believe an ex-Navy SEAL over the word of a Stock-holm Syndrome hostage, but you go ahead and roll those dice."

"Thor."

"Yes, that was me. He'll be stuck in traffic right about now. It'll be at least three hours before he figures this out, but we'll be gone. And if you do anything fucked up whatsoever, I'm going to have the cops in there so fast—you understand?"

I glared over his shoulder at the sidewalk. That was all the answer he'd get from me.

"Hands on the wheel."

I complied, mind whirling with fear.

He grabbed my purse and rummaged through it. Going through my purse. Oh, I wanted this guy to *die*.

My heart raced as I discarded one idea for vanquishing him after another. He had me hostage in the worst way. He could bring us all down so fast.

He pulled out a stick of lipstick and handed it to me.

"You're going to write a message," he said. "On the rearview mirror."

"What?" I asked, horrified.

"*I can't take it anymore. I'm sorry*," he dictated. "I'd have you write more, but the space is a bit limited."

Just like their first girlfriend, Venus—she'd written that lipstick message on the bathroom mirror just before she went off and killed herself. "I won't do that to them."

"I think you will."

"Fuck you," I hissed, thinking lavishly of the guns strapped up and down my leg.

"That's exactly what Venus said."

My mouth fell open in shock.

He made a big mock frown, more a smile-frown. "All this time, the poor tortured gods."

My heart pounded.

Robert Manning had killed Venus? She hadn't killed herself

after all? My guys had felt responsible for her death. It had nearly broken them—especially Zeus. All those years of guilt over her suicide. I wanted to gouge this asshole's eyes out of their sockets for what he'd put my guys through.

"They know I'd never write that. They won't buy it."

"That's not the point I'm trying to make to them. The point, the lesson I have for them, is that they could've prevented this if they hadn't let their emotions get away with them. If only they'd been paying more attention," he said mockingly. "If only they hadn't been so focused on vengeance."

The horror sunk in deep. That *was* what they'd say. They'd blame themselves.

"They let vengeance blind them," he continued, "even as their precious Isis begged them to pull their heads out of their asses. Vengeance never sleeps. Can't even take a nap apparently."

So he'd wired the truck.

He pressed the gun against my arm. "Write it. Or do I have to move to plan B?"

The chess moves between us became preternaturally clear at this point. I'd write the message to buy time and keep him from raising the alarm about my guys inside the bank.

He'd make me go somewhere with him in his vehicle, leaving the empty SUV with the message in it. And I'd go, just to get us the hell out of the area. Because the alternative was getting my guys busted and probably killed, and we were a pack. We watched out for each other.

We protected each other with everything.

And it wasn't as if I was helpless; I was pretty dramatically armed. But Manning would know that, too. He was smart—obviously smarter than any of us had realized. He had tactics, being a SEAL and all. And insider information.

But every one of those moves was the lesser of two evils. It was a decision tree, and I had to follow it his way if I loved my guys.

So I wrote the lipstick note to buy time, hands shaking with anger. I got out of our big tinted-windows Navigator and walked with him a half a block down to his pickup truck, even though getting into a bad guy's vehicle is the worst thing you can do, odds-wise.

But he didn't know me. He'd always looked down on me. He would underestimate me. That was my ace in the hole.

He made me take the driver's seat, his gun trained at my head. "Drive natural, or you are splat," he said.

I snorted. "A creepy thing that a creepy guy says. That's what that is."

He gave me that horrible smile-frown.

A creepy guy with stupid hair, I wanted to say, but I needed to be smart, not antagonistic.

I pulled out. He hadn't made me give up my weapons. Was it possible he was such a creep that he couldn't imagine a little lady besting him? By the time we were about four blocks away, I was really thinking about trying something, but he was watching me too closely.

"And they don't need your fucking lessons," I said.

"But they do," Manning said. "I've been with them all along. I'm like their *sensei*. Do you know what a sensei is?"

"From the context of that sentence, I'd go with *loserish jackalope*."

The fist across my jaw was sure and swift, and the pain blinded me for a split second. I drove, vision fuzzing with rage. Blood oozed inside my mouth.

"You mean that's not what it means?" I asked, refusing to let him think he'd cowed me.

"A sensei is a wise teacher. I was fighting a private war long before your three masters were."

"They're not my masters," I bit out.

"Technically, your masters are excellent at what they do, but I feel their emotional maturity isn't where it should be."

"*Their* emotional maturity?"

He jerked and I stiffened, waiting for a strike that didn't come, thankfully.

He laughed, like that was a clever gambit or something. "I see you fancy yourself as something of a teacher, too. Such as you are. Turn here," he said, indicating an on-ramp. We veered onto the highway, heading east, out of LA. "Your point about vengeance the other day, about an agency not being able to beg for mercy, I felt it was a cogent one."

"You have microphones throughout our *house*?" The idea horrified me.

He smiled. "Not microphones—your masters would find them in a second. I tweaked the security apparatus in the house to serve as a pickup for the parabolic mics outside."

I frowned. "And you framed that Travis guy."

"And Ingvey before him. If it hadn't been for their lust for that bank, they would've seen through it. Odin almost did, but he couldn't quite let go of his need for vengeance. That's this lesson, you see. Your masters need to operate from the point of logic, not emotion."

Jackalope, I thought.

"I'd say exhibit A of that point is on your arm. Everything with that tattoo is wrong. It's no wonder he had to tie you."

It took me just a few minutes to get it. "You watch, too."

I took his sneer as a yes.

My lip where he'd hit me felt huge and swollen.

I drove on with tense perfection, raging with anger, scrambling to think. Rush hour traffic was light for once. Like a horrible miracle that I didn't want.

"You're sick."

"I'm just glad I don't have A/V stuff up in the hills where they took you the other night, though I heard them planning it. That sounded like some fucked-up shit. I find it disgusting when you masturbate to that cartoon porn. You're as deviant as they are."

"We're not deviant, we're awesome," I bit out.

He directed me back onto a surface street after a while. I drove farther and farther out, past familiar strip malls full of familiar chain stores, and then past unfamiliar strip malls full of familiar chain stores.

I wondered if they'd discovered the note yet. Of course they wouldn't have; it would take them a long time to pull apart that bank. Two more hours at least, probably three or four.

It was possible Thor would get back and find it first.

My heart hurt, thinking of how distraught and enraged they'd feel.

How helpless.

I had to find a way to survive this. To get back to them.

"Where are we going?" I asked.

"Drive."

I once saw something on Reddit that you should crash a vehicle if you had somebody making you drive someplace, that the driver's side airbag would save you.

But then again, it was on Reddit.

"If they really cared about you, they would've called off the job," he said.

Okay, maybe I *would* crash the truck.

We drove past a lamppost with a massive, solid-looking base that would've been a good candidate. At the last moment, I couldn't do it.

It turns out that crashing a vehicle isn't the easiest thing to make yourself do.

"I heard Odin and Zeus talking about how uncomfortable they were that Sleazy Travis didn't confess," Manning continued. "At least their instincts are spot on. Too bad they didn't heed them. The call of vengeance was just a little too compelling. They put their passions over their reason. And didn't heed the warning."

"You sent the Abe Lincoln message?" I asked.

"Yes indeed," he said. "I gave them a chance to straighten up, but they chose not to. They chose passion and petty bullshit. Well, they'll never make that mistake again after today, and that is my lesson for them."

He crossed his legs, like we were having this casual and pleasant chat.

Creep.

"They discussed it a ton when you weren't around," he continued. "Deep down, they really weren't sure it was Travis—I could tell. Zeus didn't tell you this, but he felt they were missing something. Eventually, he decided it was just his enjoyment of investigation speaking. He was a *federale* back in the day, but of course, you know that. Even investigators lie to themselves. Love is blind, as they say. Tell me, Isis," Manning continued, modulating his voice a few octaves upwards for extra creepiness, "do you want them to love you?"

"They already do."

"Do they? I'm not so sure."

"Yeah, yeah, yeah," I said. "You're just the A/V guy. You're a camera and tape recorder, but you're not really there. I feel their love."

"I don't know about that, considering they'd rather be sitting in heating ducts and stealing things that don't belong to them than protecting you."

I sniffed, like he was so beneath everything, but if both Zeus and Odin had been having serious ongoing doubts about Sleazy Travis being the feather guy, how could they have continued with the robbery?

"We both know what they really love."

"You don't know anything."

He smiled.

I frowned at the road. They were willing to die for each other, and sure, they were willing to die for me, but Manning had a point. Vengeance was underneath it all. The foundation of everything. My eyes heated with tears.

"Poor Isis," he said in his creepy tone. "Your robbers have only one true love."

"Jealous?"

He looked smug.

Jealous? It was a sad retort. I was starting to feel like I was in third grade, desperate for a zinger but only coming up with stuff like, '*No, YOU'RE a doofus.*'

I tried not to lose hope, but I had to face facts. I was alone now, and I needed to do something. Driving into a post was foolish, but I had the feeling that at the end of this drive, I might long desperately for one foolish option as opposed to five suicidal ones.

We were going beyond the suburbs and into the exurbs now. I gazed at the signs, ignoring the feeling of him monitoring my expression.

I hated it.

I hated him.

Chapter Eighteen

"Almost there," creepy Manning said as we passed a sign for Holden Corners.

Holden Corners?

My mouth went dry.

Holden Quarry was in Holden Corners. The quarry was where Venus's body had been found.

He smiled, knowing that I was putting it together, I suppose. "The good news is that your fellas *are* able to learn the lessons I offer them. First they learned the lesson of Venus: To refrain from compromising their excellence in service of their libido. She almost got them caught on the Keustonville job some years back. I knew then that I had to act. To show them not everyone has their strength." He pointed. "Turn here."

I turned onto a street where the streetlights rose up out of fat concrete bases; it was here I decided to go for foolish. I was part of a takeover bank robbery gang.

I could do it.

At a yellow light I gunned the engine and jerked the wheel, aiming for the nearest lamp base.

It was like a slow-motion dream, watching us careen toward it.

I could feel Manning's shock as he grabbed the wheel, trying to wrest control, but I had two hands and he had just one, being that the other held a gun.

Suddenly he hit me in the chin with it.

The shattering pain so stunned me that I lost my edge—just enough for him to grab the wheel and avoid the crash.

Stars whirled around in front of my eyes.

I let up off the gas and the truck slowed. Cars behind us honked.

I was done driving right.

He pressed his gun to my belly. "You wanna drive shot? Is that what you want?"

I thought about it. Would he really do it? Something needed to interrupt this madness.

"My plan still works with you bleeding out. You think I can't shoot you and take over? It's not my favorite option, but I'll do it."

Was he bluffing? I didn't want to find out.

I sped back up and drove normally. My chin throbbed. My lip burned.

"Kudos, however," he said. "Few people can actually commit to a deliberate crash like you did—it goes against their self-preservation. Most people can't bring themselves to do it."

"Most people can't bring themselves to do it?" I said. "And here I thought it was creepy when people knew too many facts about Smurf dolls."

He gave me a hard look. "If you try it again, I *will* shoot you. If you move either of your hands from the steering wheel, that's an instant shot, too. You understand? And FYI, I know what you're packing."

Damn.

Ten minutes later he was directing me into the quarry parking lot.

Seven at night.

Deserted.

"Stop here, but keep your hands on the wheel. I have no aversion to shooting you and throwing your body off the cliff. It's not like they're really going to think you killed yourself. Your death here is more for the sake of symmetry than verisimilitude." He paused, seeming proud of his smart-sounding sentence.

It made me want to gouge out his eyes.

He made me put the truck in park and directed me to knit my fingers on top of my head, at which point he patted his creep hands up and down my legs, efficiently and clinically removing the weapons from my thigh and ankle holsters. I was glad he didn't touch me in a sexual manner, but it also showed what a fucking pro he was. Manning wasn't somebody who could be distracted in that way, even if I had the stomach for it, which I didn't.

"What do you think they're doing now?" he asked, taking my last gun out of my ankle holster, my mini nine. "What do you think?"

"I think they're coming after me," I said.

"What do you really think?"

I pictured them ravishing the safety deposit boxes. Enjoying the riches. Filling bags. Thor would be nearing the Mexican border. "I think they're coming to tear you the fuck apart." It was more a wish than a possibility, but I wished it fervently.

"They don't know you're gone yet, that's what I think. I have alerts set up for when they get into that SUV. Don't you wish you could hear them when they discover the message you wrote?"

"No."

He grinned. "I do. And I'll get my wish, because it'll be recorded. They'll want to rip me apart. You can console yourself with that. They'll get a real vengeance hit off that. They'll drive here pretty fucking fast. I'd let you stick around to listen to them discover your message and what they say on the drive, but I don't like to cut things that close. Suffice to say it'll be entertaining. Nothing like the grand finale, though. Don't you wish you could be a fly on the stone when they discover your body in the quarry right where Venus's body was?"

I looked away, chin and lip both throbbing like mad. I wouldn't give him the satisfaction of a reaction.

He motioned with his gun. "Out."

I weighed my options, feeling like I was in a nightmare maze with no way out.

"Out, or I shoot you and carry you. Or more, drag you. You're too heavy to carry."

My pulse whooshed in my ears, and I wondered dimly if he was trying to insult me by suggesting I was heavy. As if a man can get more insulting than *wanting you dead.*

"Out."

I started working off my heels, pushing them off with my toes. As soon as they were off, I leaned on the horn. The blare echoed off the stone piles, filling the area with sound.

Manning cursed and went for the keys.

That was my chance. I jumped out of the truck and ran for it. The rocks felt hard on my feet, and one or two definitely pierced the skin, but torn-up feet were better than broken ankles.

What are torn-up feet also better than? Death.

I ran like hell toward the nearest massive pile of stones, huge enough to cover half a tennis court and maybe five stories tall.

I heard him swear behind me, but it was a good sign that he hadn't liked the honking—he was worried somebody might hear. Maybe he'd be reluctant to use the gun. He did have that silencer, but a silenced gun isn't that silent.

I made it around to the far side of the mountain of stones and stilled.

The sharp little stones were a bitch to walk on.

On the upside, I could hear the crunch of his footfalls as he reached the other side of the pile.

He paused there.

I waited for his next move, senses on alert. Suddenly he was on the run again, his footsteps going clockwise.

I moved the same way, keeping the pile in between us, holding up the hem of my dress. The bottoms of my feet were raw and probably bloody, but unlike Manning, I could walk in relative silence. He picked up his pace to a run and so did I.

How long I could keep the pile between us? A pretty long time, I was thinking.

I heard him slow on the other side, and then stop, and then he headed the other way.

I mirrored his movements. As long as the pile was between us, I was safe.

After a while of chasing around, I picked up a large rock and tossed it clear over the pile at him. "An asshole loser A/V guy! With stupid hair!"

Not exactly productive, but what did I have to lose?

He moved clockwise, trying to come after me more stealthily, but I could hear him. If I kept it up long enough, my guys could get to me. It could be three hours, maybe four or five until they discovered the message. Could I make it?

Damn right!

We chased around back and forth. I felt like maybe an hour passed, though maybe it was ten minutes. I thought about alternate plans—climbing to the top, or burying myself as a way to hide, but nothing seemed as effective as keeping a giant motherfucking pile of stones between us.

Then there came a silence that went on a little too long. I waited until I caught a flash of green out the corner of my eye.

Crap!

I bolted away; a nearby spray of stones told me that his shot just missed me.

He'd taken off his shoes. We were now at the same stealth level.

It got harder to keep the pile between us after that. He'd chase around and just appear and I'd have to take off, but sometimes he'd change directions and come at me the other way. He could never quite catch me, but I was feeling tired and a little freaked out. Dusk was falling, too, which made it harder to see him.

It was when I was on the side of the pile that was nearest to his truck that I got the idea to go back there. It was a lot of tundra to cross, but the rock pile strategy felt less promising, now.

I ran for it.

I heard another shot, but I kept going.

Zeus had once told me that it was nearly impossible to hit a target while you were running, which I'm sure he was.

Miraculously, I got to the truck and found the door open. I went in and looked around. Where were my guns? I could hear him coming. With shaking hands, I searched under the seats, yanked open the glove compartment.

What had he done with my guns? He couldn't be carrying them all!

He was nearing. I jumped out and shut the door, hiding behind the truck just as I'd hid behind the rock pile.

"Lose something?" he asked from the other side, voice disturbingly close.

I crouched there on the other side of the door, pulse racing. Well, fuck it. As long as I could keep the vehicle between us, I was safe. I just had to survive for the next minute, and then the minute after that.

"I threw them into the grass," he said. "Over behind the pole."

I looked out at the weedy patch at the base of a utility pole at the edge of the lot, about ten parking spaces away. I caught the glint of metal, but it would be suicide to go for it.

"You know you can't get away," he said in his creep voice.

"Maybe not, but I can outlast you."

"Actually, you can't. This isn't the rock pile, honey. All I have to do is jump up on the hood."

"I'll crawl under then," I said, shaking deep down.

"And I'll jump down and shoot you," he said.

Wildly, I thought this scenario through. Yeah, he could do that.

I felt shaky, breath ragged, a cornered animal tasting her own death.

"Checkmate," he added smugly.

Again I eyed the grass patch.

"Now, all I want to do is take a little walk with you," he continued. "Do I drag your bloody corpse, or do you walk with me?"

"Drag my bloody corpse, jackhole!"

The vehicle rocked, and I knew he was getting on top of it.

I scrambled underneath, moving on pure fear. *Survive just one more minute,* I told myself. One more minute. Add one minute to another. Add that minute to another.

The truck bounced above me again. Was he on the move? Which side would he come at me from? I scrambled toward the front and something caught my dress, scraping my back. I kept on —the front was the least likely side he'd come at me from, I'd decided. Sometimes you have to go forward until you can't. Sometimes that's the only option you get.

It was then that I heard the rumble of a nearby engine and the spit of rocks under tires. Somebody else was here. Would they die, too? I just kept crawling under the car toward the front. Maybe he'd already jumped off. Maybe he was crouching on the ground, aiming at me.

Brakes squealed. Doors opened.

And somebody—or something—yelled. *Roared.* The sound was very nearly inhuman.

Yet there was something wonderfully familiar about it. My heart pounded.

Something crunched the gravel—or more like tore it up. I peered out under the bumper and caught sight of big black boots pounding past in the direction of the rock pile...I scooted closer and saw that it was Zeus, chasing Manning to the rock pile. Odin appeared, chasing after them. They were both still in their black bank-robbing clothes.

A voice nearby called out. "Isis?"

Thor.

"I'm under here," I sobbed. "Thor!"

Tennis shoes appeared.

"I got her!" Thor yelled. "She's with me!"

His knees and then his face appeared, shaggy blond hair hanging sideways like the most beautiful thing in the world. "Goddess," he said, stretching his arm under the truck toward me. "You're okay. We're here."

"He's out there," I whispered.

"Not for long." He got down on his belly to be face-to-face with me. "You're okay," he said softly. He came under with me, right next to me, and wrapped his arms around me. "We gotcha."

I burst out crying, big ugly sobs into his shoulder. "He was going to throw me into the pit! And you were in traffic—"

"Shhh." He tightened his arms around me, pulling me close in the cramped, dark, oil-smelling space. "Shhh." He held me there on the sharp stones.

"I thought you wouldn't come," I whispered.

"Of course we came. Are you hurt anywhere?"

"I don't know! Kind of. But not really."

"Come on out, goddess."

I just held onto him, not wanting to move.

"Will you come out, goddess?"

I didn't get how traumatized I was until that second. I knew that with Odin and Zeus after him, Manning wouldn't come for me, but I still felt frightened. *You're okay,* I told myself, making myself scramble out with him. Thor helped me up. An angry shadow crossed his eyes as he got a good look at my chin where Manning hit me, then he pulled me into his arms.

"I'm so sorry," he whispered into my ear. "I should never have left you."

"You thought Lupe needed you."

"*You* needed me. It's on all of us that we didn't figure things out." He pulled back and touched my chin. "He did this?"

"Yeah. Nothing broken."

"Where else are you hurt?"

"My back. My feet."

"Come on." He picked me up and carried me back toward our SUV. "We were so worried," he said.

"How did you figure it out?"

"Odin called about twenty minutes after I took off. He and Zeus were feeling wrong about the whole situation. Going ahead with these questions about Sleazy Travis being our guy—it was reckless. So Odin turned on his phone and called me, just to check in. He was freaked that I wasn't with you. I texted Lupe a trick question. She texted me back, and I knew it wasn't her." He opened the back of the vehicle and settled me onto the end. He grabbed a soft blanket and wrapped me up and slid in next to me. There was eerie silence all around the quarry. "They got out of there and went to the Nav and found the message. I got there a little later. God, when we saw that mirror—"

"He made me write it."

"I know." Tenderly, he touched my cheek and looked into my eyes. "We all knew."

"Thank you," I said.

He snorted, like that was ridiculous, me thanking him. "We should be begging for your forgiveness, goddess. We were putting vengeance over what's really important," he said. "The Prime, it's just some bank. Fuck the Prime Royale. Fuck ZOX. What matters is our family."

I took a lock of his bright blond hair between two fingers, loving him outrageously. "He killed Venus," I said.

Thor's blue eyes glittered darkly. "And I believe he's paying right about now."

"They'll kill him."

"Well...eventually."

I shuddered. "He was Lincoln," I added.

"We figured."

"So...they just left the Prime open and unburgled?"

"Nah, Matteo pulled the Gigis in. So he's the fucking hero. Those girls are shit at takeovers, but they can crack a safe. They'll get into those boxes."

"You won't get the jewels. The revenge on ZOX—they won't know—"

"Vengeance isn't as important as you. As us all staying together," Thor said.

I began to tear up. I'd needed to hear that so badly.

"Hey, it's okay." Thor held me. "I'm sorry I left you."

I mashed my face into his soft shirt, breathing him in. "You had to help Lupe." A crunch of stones sounded from the direction of the rock pile. The crunches sped up—two pairs of feet. I didn't have to look to know who it was.

"She's okay," Thor called.

I turned to look.

Zeus was ahead of Odin, eyes shining like diamonds in his sweaty face. A violent smudge of mud glistened on his cheekbone, and as he neared, I realized that it was blood. Odin was behind him, dark hair tousled, hard planes of his face set in a glowering mask.

"Goddess." Zeus mashed into me, holding me against his big, solid body. I circled my arms around him, taking comfort in his hulking strength and heaving breath.

Odin came in on the other side of me, grabbed the back of my head, and kissed me on the cheek. "Goddess," he said, cramming halfway into Zeus. "I'm so sorry," he said when our gazes locked. "We were such *fucking-g* fools, hypnotized by the jewels and vengeance."

"But you came," I said.

"We should've never left," Odin said, eyeing my chin. "There is so *fucking-g* much we should've seen."

"Forgive us." Zeus slid a gentle palm over my shoulder, his expression a strange mixture of joy and grief. "You are more precious than anything in that bank," he said. "And we almost lost you. Do you know what that would've done? Do you know how much we love you, goddess?"

For once I was speechless.

Thor took my hand. "We love you. We realized we'd never even told you that while we were racing over here."

My heart nearly flew out of my chest.

"We love you. I love you," Thor said.

"I *fucking-g* love you beyond anything," Odin said.

"I love you, too," I said, looking from Thor to Zeus to Odin. "I love all of you and each of you. Like wildfire."

Odin's voice sounded gravelly, serious. "We don't deserve that love right now—"

"You're wrong," I said. "You always do."

"No, Odin's right," Zeus said. "We don't deserve it right now. But we are going to spend however long it takes making this up to you."

"Because you are everything precious to us," Odin said.

My eyes went to the rock pile. "Manning—"

"He's dead," Zeus said.

"Good," I whispered.

"We ripped him apart. Literally," Zeus growled. "Odin ripped his guts out."

I shifted my eyes to Odin and I knew from his expression that it was true. Also, his black shirt was wet with blood. Zeus's clothes were bloody, too.

"You want to see his body?" Zeus asked.

"Umm...that's okay," I said. "I'm just going to believe you."

He looked disappointed. "But it might be good, psychologically, to have seen his corpse with your own eyes so you know deep down that he can't hurt you again."

It was sweet, but also a little bit morbid. "That's okay."

Zeus's expression hardened. "Nobody fucks with the God Pack."

"Right," I said, feeling a sudden hopelessness at the reminder of their lust for vengeance.

"No, it's different now," Odin said. "Vengeance needs to be a choice, not a compulsion."

"Except for killing Manning," Zeus said. "That was kind of a compulsion for me, but now that he's dead, vengeance can be a choice."

"So we're going to the island?" I teased. "To retire in splendor?"

"No," Zeus said. "That still sounds just sad. The point is, we're not the bitches of vengeance anymore."

"Never again," Thor said.

Ironically, I had twisted sensei Robert Manning to thank for that.

"You guys are amazing," I said. Because really, this was huge.

Right in that moment, they seemed completely free, like wild animals.

Bloody.

Primal.

Beautiful.

Intensely alive.

Chapter Nineteen

THREE WEEKS LATER, MY GUYS AND I WERE LOUNGING on the porch in our matching plush bathrobes after some exuberant fun in the hot tub. The last remnant of my struggle with Manning, my chin bruise, was nearly all the way faded. You could barely see it.

Zeus set down his paperback novel and stood. "Who wants lemonade?"

I smiled up at him. "Could it be strawberry lemonade?"

"Could be and will be." He headed inside.

Getting kidnapped, chased, and nearly tossed to your death in a quarry pit turned out to be quite the boon if you were the type who liked being waited on hand and foot by three hunky bank robbers.

Which I was.

But it went so much deeper than that. The experience changed us. I got this new appreciation for my guys. Out there in the quarry parking lot with them all bloody and invigorated, I came to love them in a newer, deeper way.

And they had a different relationship with vengeance, too.

They were no longer the bitches of vengeance, just like Zeus had promised.

They might still want to rob banks, they assured me, and they would strike back if ZOX came after them, but they didn't *have* to do any of it. Odin was doing more painting these days. Thor was into his clinic work.

Zeus announced he was opening a detective agency.

"What?" Odin said. "You're opening a detective agency?"

"Yeah, why not?" Zeus said. "I put it out on the grapevine already."

"Don't detectives catch criminals?" I asked. "And work with the police?" Both of those were rhetorical questions.

Thor was laughing. "Are you thinking this through? You start busting criminals, you'll never get served at Guvvey's again. And that will be the least of your problems."

"No, this detective agency would help criminals. Our peeps need detectives, too," Zeus said. "In fact, we have our first client."

Odin sat up. "You don't think you should've consulted the gang?"

Zeus shrugged. "If you don't want to solve this guy's mystery, I'll do it myself."

Odin grumbled. "Of course I want to help solve a mystery. Who is it?"

"Alexander Hamilton." Zeus pulled out his phone. "Obviously not his real name." He hit play on a voicemail and a man's voice filled the room.

Yeah, this is...Alexander Hamilton calling. So...somebody out there framed me up for something. Made me a powerful enemy. This frame-up was tight. They thought of everything. And I really need you to, you know, to figure out who did it so I can have a chat with this person if you know what I mean. I'm around this week. Shoot me a time and place and I'll be there.

Odin narrowed his eyes. "Shit," he said.

"What?" Zeus said. "You recognize the voice?"

"That's Herk Washington, man," Odin said.

Thor sat up. "*The* Herk Washington? Why would he be calling us?"

"Obviously he got framed for something and needs our help," Zeus said.

At the moment, however, we were enjoying the quiet evening. I was busy knitting wee little socks to send along with the fabulous baby gifts we'd picked out for Lupe, who had given birth to a healthy baby boy just the week before.

We'd had the security system and cameras ripped out and replaced. It was so creepy to know Manning had been watching us all that time. He'd messed up the robbery for my guys, of course, though Matteo and the Gigis had made out like bandits—the jewels in the Prime Royale went beyond everybody's wildest dreams. Those four were off living it up in various glamorous capitals around the world as they dealt with different black-market brokers. Macy hadn't forgiven Matteo on a personal level, but they were working together again; it gave Matteo a chance to prove himself. Hopefully he would.

Before they'd left, Matteo and the Gigis had dropped by and handed over a chunk of the haul as a gift for us having done so much of the prep work. It was a lovely gesture, and now we were more fabulously wealthy than ever.

Zeus came back with a pitcher of strawberry lemonade and glasses. He'd changed into jeans, and the tattoo on his arm seemed to glow in the moonlight. I studied it as he poured the lemonade into the glasses.

You WISH we were dead, motherfuckers.

I reached out and ran my finger over it. "I can't believe I used to think it was so negative. It means something new for me now."

"Like what?" Odin asked.

"I can't explain it," I said. "The words are the same, but everything else is different. It's just more beautiful somehow."

Odin's eyes shone with pride. "It means we love each other," he said.

"And that we're a family," Zeus said.

"Forever," Thor said. "To support each other in our desires, whatever they might be."

I looked at the tattoo, emblazoned on the arm of one of the men I loved. To me it meant all that and more. It contained every possibility in the world.

~ The End ~

Thank you for reading the bank robbers!! I hope you love them as much as I do.

&

What's next for the God Pack?

I nearly keel over from shock when my guys' mortal enemy, ruthless Agent Denko, calls them by their real names and spills their deepest, darkest secrets—including few things they didn't even know about each other.

Luckily, Odin has the man tied up at the time, and he's able to slap some duct tape over his mouth. Denko is clearly trying to tear us apart.

Is he succeeding?

Does he know something that we don't?

My guys are the most protective and dangerous men alive, but who will protect us from the truth about each other?

Or will the truth make us fiercer and more fabulous than ever?

Grab The Most Wanted, available at your favorite bookseller.

&

"If I could I would give 10 more stars. I thought this was such a fantastic and thrilling book. Oh and let us not forget THAT scene."
~Amazon

Also by Annika Martin

THE BANK ROBBERS

Spicy reverse harem: read in order

The Hostage Bargain

The Wrong Idea

The Deeper Game

The Most Wanted

The Hard Way

The Best Trick

BILLIONAIRES OF MANHATTAN

Stand-alone romantic comedy: read in any *order*

Most Eligible Billionaire

The Billionaire's Wake-up-call Girl

Breaking The Billionaire's Rules

The Billionaire's Fake Fiancée

Return Billionaire to Sender

Just Not That Into Billionaires

Butt-dialing the Billionaire

DANGEROUS ROYALS

Dark and edgy mafia romance; read in order

Dark Mafia Prince

Wicked Mafia Prince

Savage Mafia Prince

Annika Martin writes in many genres; find a complete list of her books,
audiobooks, and translated works at www.annikamartinbooks.com

All the Annika deets!

Annika Martin is a New York Times bestselling author who lives in Minneapolis with her non-bank-robber husband. In her spare time she enjoys taking pictures of her cats, consuming boatloads of chocolate suckers, and tending her wild, bee-friendly garden.

newsletter:
http://annikamartinbooks.com/newletter

TikTok:
@annikamartinauthor

Facebook:
www.facebook.com/AnnikaMartinBooks

Instagram:
instagram.com/annikamartinauthor

website:
www.annikamartinbooks.com

Reader group of awesomeness
www.facebook.com/groups/AnnikaMartinFabulousGang/

Q: Did the bank robbers leave you satisfied? Desperately yearning? Saddled with a mysterious cartoon porn addiction?

A. Whatever the answer, I'm always so grateful when people leave reviews, even just a line or two. It helps readers find the books and it super helps the series.

PS: Odin sends kisses!

The bank robbers thank you for reading.